FRAZIER

A CROSS TO BEAR Book 3

KATHI S. BARTON

World Castle Publishing, LLC
Pensacola, Florida
Copyright © Kathi S. Barton 2023
Hardback ISBN: 9798388217264
Paperback ISBN: 9781960076489
eBook ISBN: 9781960076496
First Edition World Castle Publishing, LLC, March 27, 2023
http://www.worldcastlepublishing.com
Licensing Notes
Cover: Karen Fuller
Editor: Karen Fuller

Chapter 1

Amelia gave the list of things that had been Phil's to the council. They weren't happy about the fact that it went to non-witches, but she didn't give a rat's ass. Phil, as they had wanted, was dead — which he was — and he wasn't going to be hurting anyone ever again.

"Once you found out where he was, why didn't you take care of him later when they weren't around." She told them that everything still would have gone to them as they were the ones that had found him. "You could have taken care that it didn't go to them somehow, couldn't you? I mean, that's a great deal of money, and we'll get no part of it as they're not witches."

"Is that what this is about? You couldn't pad your own money with his? Christ, no wonder it's getting more and more difficult to keep witches from turning to the dark side. At least they don't have to pay you guys when they make a little money on the side." Number two told her to be civil to them as they were her council. "Perhaps you are, but that doesn't mean I have to agree with you. And as usual, I don't. The money has been given to them, and they're the rightful owners of it. It's done."

It wasn't, not really. The money was still in her possession, but the magic had been given to them. Unbeknownst to her, the entire family got the magic. There certainly was more than enough to go around. But she didn't tell them that nor the fact that she'd been given a boost too. If they had gotten their heads out of their asses and not thought about themselves for a change, they should have noticed it. As it was now, she thought she could take them on and come out on top. Instead, she just let them talk among themselves about the injustice of the magic not coming to them. Then the five of them looked at her.

"We've made a decision." She was just pissed

off enough to ask them what it was going to cost her. "Good that you're on board with us. We'll take half your monies — there is a great deal of it, we know and have your magic spread out between the six of us. That way, we are compensated for your mistake."

"What mistake would that be? The fact that you assigned me to make sure that Phil was no longer around, and I did that? Or the mistake I made in coming here to tell you the truth. Either way, you're not getting shit from me or my magic. Also, and this might surprise you, too, I don't give a shit if you were compensated or not. Not that you deserve anything, but you're not going to get anything from me." All she did was lift her hand, and the five of them disappeared. "Christ, love a duck." She dropped to the floor.

"Hello, Amelia." Amelia didn't move from her position on the floor, not even to look up when she heard the woman speaking above her. It wasn't that she didn't know who it was. She just decided that she had better be paying her respects today. "Oh, do get up from there and talk to me. It's been decades since I've had a conversation with you. Come now, get up."

Not moving from the floor, she noticed that the

five men that made up the witches' council were gone. Not even the large elaborate desk they'd been sitting in was there any longer. Lying her head back on the floor, she spoke to the voice of the woman in the room with her.

"I didn't kill them, did I?" She still hadn't moved from the floor but raised her head just enough to look at the woman standing before her. "Mom, you look amazing. What have you been doing with yourself?"

"Thinking. Get up, Amelia. You're going to make me get a crick in my neck like this, and I do need to speak to you." She stood up, and a table and two chairs appeared beside her. "We're having tea. Well, I am. You're having some juice. In answer to your question, yes, they're all five dead. You killed them, so when you leave here, I'd expect to take yourself someplace where you can rest. You won't need to hide, darling. They've been causing trouble for far too long, anyway. Their magic, pitiful as it was, will come to you as well. You need to be prepared for it."

"I told you before, I'm fine with what I have now." They sat, and two under witches came to serve them. Not only were there several kinds of juice that she could choose from but there were fresh sandwiches and tea for her mother. "Why didn't you do something about the five of them before today? I told you they were taking money that didn't belong to them. Why today?"

"You were here to make sure that I can't be blamed for their demise. You won't either. I think that everyone will be thrilled to know that they're dead. But with me being the grand witch, there would have had to be an investigation as well as an inquiry about shit. I'm not in the mood to go through all that. The way you took care of them will suffice the others more than adequately, I think. How have you been, darling?" She told her that she'd been great. "I'm so happy to hear that. I've been looking ahead—I know that you hate when I do that, but I've seen that you're to have a mate soon."

"You've said that to me before, mom. And my answer hasn't changed in all this time. I don't want a mate, and I have no need for one. I've seen how mates can destroy each other enough for several lifetimes of meanness and pettiness. I'm not going to allow anyone to treat me less than I deserve to be treated.

Like a person, not a dishrag." She told her that this man would never do that to her. "I'm sure you'd like to think that, but all men are dirtballs, and we both know it. Remember my father? He was jealous of everything you did. Even though he could have been better himself, he had too much fun making us feel bad for our ambition and worth."

Her father had been gone so long that she couldn't remember his voice, much less his face anymore. Amelia couldn't even remember the last time she'd been to his garden to talk to him, either. The faeries took care of it all the time, and since she and her father had never been close, she just stopped going to talk to him. It would have been the same way when he'd been alive, she thought with a little laugh. All one-sided. Though it would have been hers this time.

"I will agree that he was a terrible role model for you, but not all men are like him. It took me a few hundred years to figure that out on my own as well." She said that most were. "Perhaps you would know that better than me as I rarely have contact with anyone but you. However, you've met his brothers. And their wives." She had to think about what she was saying and stood up twice before sitting back down on the chair.

"Mom, you don't mean that I'm going to be mated to one of the Cross bears, do you?" Her mom smiled and nodded. Telling her that she was brilliant in the way she'd figured that out on her own. "I don't think you understand how powerful they are in their own right. Not to mention the whole thing about me not wanting a mate. I'm sure I've explained that to you before, correct?" Her mother never listened to her when it came to what she wanted for her. She was as… well, as stubborn as she was at times.

"Sure you do. You just need to meet the right man. His name is Frazier. Such a good strong name, don't you think? And he works with the elements of the earth when he works with his artistry. I'm not sure that he understands that he and the earth are a great deal alike, but you should see some of his work. Amelia, he's a brilliant man, and he loves the earth as much as you do." She didn't bother speaking to her mom about it. She knew her feelings about having a mate. "He and his family will need you in the very near future, child. He, along with one of his brothers, will be dreadfully murdered if you don't accept my word on this. As soon as you do, he'll have all the power he needs to survive what is coming his way."

"Just fix it, so he's all right without me being his mate. You can do that, can't you? For your only child? Mom, do you have any idea how much I've worked at being single." She nodded at her. "Then you understand why I won't do this. Just fix it up for them, and I'll go about my merry little way. You and I will pretend that this conversation never happened. What do you think about that?"

"I'm dying, Amelia. I want to die, but it's coming to me faster than I had thought when I made plans with the earth to bring the two of you together. You must listen to me when I tell you that Frazier will be a great man to you and not a better mate to have around either." She asked her what she was talking about, fearful of what her mom might say to her. "I've been around longer than most of the earth, and its creatures, child. You know this. I am exhausted. More so than I've ever been. My magic, while strong, is boring to me too. Without a mate here, I have no one I can depend on. I know I can depend on you, but even that is becoming too much for me. I'm lonely and bored to pieces, child."

"As you said, you can depend on me. I come to you every time you call for me, don't I? I'll always be here for you, Mom. I've said that to you before. Just call, and I'll be right here for you." She said that it wasn't the same. She had no one to share with. "Of course you do. You can share with me."

As soon as the words left her mouth, Amelia realized her mistake. Giving her mom the opening she'd been waiting for, Amelia knew she was going to be in big trouble. Her mom took her hand into hers, and the magic poured over her. Even as she was overpowered with her mom's considerable magic, she could see the trouble that a man she thought was Frazier was going to be killed in. As soon as it occurred to her who he was, the magic pulled him to safety along with his brother.

Christ, she was going to have to sleep for years at the rate that the magic was coming to her. The magic and the knowledge that came with it made her head spin around. She was, at one point, sick with it. Just as she was thinking that it might be coming to an end, where the magic was all shared with her, another wave of it hit her, taking her under and out.

Waking up, she was in her old bedroom in her mother's home. Sitting up, she sat there for several seconds until her head or the room, she wasn't sure which it was, stopped spinning. Her body ached as well. Painfully in places that she'd forgotten existed on a person.

Finally thinking that she could move without falling over, she made her way into the hall to find her mom. Damn it, there was going to be hell to pay when she found her. She'd tricked her, plain and simple. Instead of finding her mom, Amelia found one of the under witches that worked for her.

"Where is she?" She bowed before her and told her she'd been lain to rest. "No, I mean…what do you mean she's been laid to rest? She wasn't to leave me right now. Where is my mom?"

"Your mother left you a message, my lady. Shall I bring it to you?" Amelia asked her to take her to her mother and bring her the note there. "She is in the faerie garden not far from here. As per her magic, once she had transferred the magic to you, she was magically put into the garden where she could rest until eternity. Also, per her wishes, she is not near your father. He is on the outer rim of the castle here so that he'd not disturb her during her resting time."

The garden was just where she'd been told it would be. There were fresh flowers, most of them bachelor buttons, her mom's favorite flower, around the small stone that marked her passing. The note she'd left for her only said that she loved her dearly and that she hoped that she'd be as happy as she was at this moment.

The stone was cold. However, she didn't take her hand away once she touched it. Asking her what she'd done to her, Amelia cried. Her heart was broken. Her mother was gone, and she'd been given the magic that had all been hers. Also, her title of the grand witch. Another thing that she hadn't wanted but was now in charge of.

Amelia decided it was time for her to go and see her mate. There was very little she could do but to take him on now. Simply because she didn't want a man in her life didn't negate the fact that she had one. Her mother had always been tricky, but Amelia thought this was her biggest slick trick of all time.

~*~

Frazier didn't speak to anyone as they made sure that Ewing, his youngest brother, was all right. He was still having trouble wrapping his mind about what he'd seen as well as felt when they'd been in the cave that— Frazier didn't let his mind go there for now. He was outside of what had been a cave, and he was alive. As was his little brother.

There were other people with them. A large group who had needed the two of them to help on the walk. They were visiting the mountain top where the first settlers had been. Their mark of time they'd spent up here was about his favorite part of tours in the summer. Frazier had been glad for the extra hands of his brother, too, when everything went to shit because of two men that wanted to cause some trouble below them.

"Other than a few scratches, you both seem to be all right. The people, for the most part, are all right too. Scared, as you can well imagine, but it could have been a good deal worse, I'm thinking." Nodding at Mark, afraid to open his mouth for fear of what would spew out, he didn't even look up when he said his name. "Something more happened than the mountainside falling in on your group, I'm assuming. Do you want to talk about it?"

A bubble of laughter spilled from his mouth, and he closed his lips tightly, so he didn't appear insane. At this point, he was starting to doubt his sanity. Mark didn't leave him but sat there on the ground with him while he tried to gather a sense of what had happened and what he'd seen when everything went to shit. He did ask about the people that had been above them on the hillside.

"Both dead. Not because of the landslide they caused but because the TNT they were using to make the mountain come down exploded before they could get away. They wanted to split the mountain in two to get to the treasures they were sure were in there. The police are handling notifying their next of kin as well as the things that they left behind. When they're satisfied with what they could get out of their bodies, they'll turn them over to us. Not that I think it will—" Another burble of laughter before Mark spoke again. He then asked about the others in their party, the families that had been with him and Ewing on the trail that they'd been walking with them. "If you're going to keep asking me the same questions over and over, this is going to take a lot longer than I thought. All are fine. One has a broken arm. They said that you tossed the man out of the cave when he seemed to freeze up. Also, cuts and bruises that will fade. I doubt their memories of this will fade, so—"

"There was a woman there. Not with us, but I saw her when I suddenly had this extra strength. Magic too. I could feel it even as I was feeling my last breath leave my body." He looked at Mark. "I should be dead. All of us should have been dead the way that happened so quickly. To be honest, I'm not entirely sure why I'm not. That big assed bolder hit me on the head, and I could feel my life slipping away then I saw her." Mark didn't say anything. Over the last several days, they'd all gotten some magic from the *kid* Phil. He'd been hoarding black magic and money since well before their grandparents were born. Playing around with the magic couldn't have prepared Frazier for the surge he'd gotten about an hour ago. "She's my mate. I don't know why I know that, but she's my other half. And she's a witch."

"Amelia? I don't know her last name, but she

was just over at the house the other day. She's very
beautiful. Earthy too. I'm not sure why that word
popped into my head when thinking about her, but
that's what I'm thinking." He said that was her. Frazier
then told him what he knew about her. "Grand witch?
I didn't know they were real. I mean, I would guess
now that I have time to think about it that it makes
sense. There would need to be someone in charge of
their group."

"It's called a Coven. And her mother passed
away, leaving all her magic to the two of us. Amelia is
very old too. Several thousand years old. Much older
than grannie and grandda are. Again, I don't know
why I know this, but the information is simply right
there for me to pick up." Mark nodded. "Is that all
you have to say about what I just told you? I'm only
here because her mother decided to give her daughter
all she was, and it saved me and Ewing, along with
those other people, is to nod at me? You do know that
this isn't anything that happens every day, don't you?
Shouldn't you be, I don't know, Christ, happy that
we're still here? I'm barely hanging on here, Mark."

"Honestly, Frazier, you don't look like you're

hanging on at all but over the deep edge of shit. What do you want? Do you want me to be upset that you're still here and not dead? Or that Ewing is all right? I'm sorry, but I can't do that. I'm thrilled to death about all of this. If she had turned you into a toadstool to save you, I'd be just fine with that as well. Damn it, Frazier. Calm down and tell me when will we all get to welcome her to the family?" Frazier simply looked over his brother's shoulder, and there she was. It was almost as if he could feel her coming near him. Mark turned to look as well and stood up when he did. "Hello again, Amelia. I'm so glad to welcome you to the family."

"My mother is dead. She died so that I could save my mate. I'm not very thrilled about shit right now." Mark laughed, and they both turned to look at him. "You think this is funny? That my mother is dead? I have news for you right now, buster. I'd gladly kill any one of you to bring her back."

"I'm so profoundly sorry for your loss, Amelia. But I will be forever thankful that you were able to save my brothers from certain death." He got down on his knees and put out his hands. "I pledge to you my undying gratitude. I am forever yours in anything that you wish from me. Except for harming my family."

"I don't want a mate. I don't…Christ, I told her I didn't want one, so I could go on with my life." Frazier cocked his head and tried to figure out what she meant by that. "I will not be ruled by you, Frazier. I swear I'll die before I give up any part of my life you demand of me."

"You think I'm going to make you do something that you don't wish? Or to ask you to do things that will make your life miserable? I'd never do that. You have it on the word of my grandparents' hearts that I'd never do anything to harm you in any way. And I do believe that it would harm you terribly if I were to even suggest that you were to give up your magic." Amelia told him that she didn't believe him. "That's all right too. Painful, I will admit, I won't lie to you, but I can understand you're not trusting me. We were thrust together by magic, strong magic, too, if I don't miss my bet, and it'll take us both time to get used to it. But as far as you being able to go on with your life, Amelia, I have no intentions of taking that away from you. I might well enjoy hanging out with you, too, if you were to allow it."

She sat down on the ground and then stood up. A table and four chairs appeared beside them, and she told them to get up off the ground. In a matter of seconds, not only did another chair appear, but Jamie and Sunny joined them at the table. Neither of which seemed the least bit put out that they'd been brought here.

They were in the middle of the woods with the nicest table and chairs sitting atop a lovely floral rug he'd ever seen. With tea and, if he didn't miss his bet, scones too being served up by who, for some reason, he knew to be lesser witches. Amelia told him there was no reason for them to be uncivilized when he asked if this was normal for her.

While she answered questions from the women as they ate and drank their treats, Mark took him to the medics that had been dropped in by helicopter. There was going to be a big fucking mess to clean up—Well, perhaps not that big. Only the road would be cleared up so that travel could be made through here. The rest would be left where it had stopped.

Several hundred tons of rocks and other debris

had traveled down the mountainside, and it hadn't cared what it took with it on its way down to the waterway below. Frazier knew that in a few years, it wouldn't be noticed that it was a newer landslide than the hundreds that had happened before today. The land would move on around it as if it had been put there for the sole purpose of making new growth.

Frazier was sitting where he'd been told even after he was given a healthy check-up from the team. They were still keeping an eye on him when Amelia joined him when he was just thinking about how he would be taking the next couple of days off to rest up. He'd already been told that by Mark. The department head at the park told him that was what he was going to be doing as well. Resting.

"You're all right then?" Frazier nodded at Amelia, and she sat down on the stone that he'd been on. "I'm sorry for the way that I spoke to you before. I'm not nearly as bitchy as I was then. Most of the time, but I didn't need to take my shitty mood out on you. But with losing my mom today and knowing that you'd been in the cave when it went down, I didn't feel like I was supposed to be nice. Not that I am usually, but today has been a shitty day all around. I ask you for your forgiveness and tell you that I'll try very hard not to take it out on you from now on. I said I'd try because I usually take my moods out on anyone around me when I'm pissed off." They both laughed a little.

"I'm still reeling from the cave incident too. I can't call it a near-death thing, as that's just too much for my mind to take in. If you'd not received her magic and passed it on to me, I'm not sure…I am sure that we'd not have survived in there. None of us would have. So I have to be thankful for that. However, I am sorry about your mother. I've never met her, but if she raised you, then she couldn't have been all that bad, right?" She laughed and said her mother had given up on her decades ago to be anything but what you see today. "Yes, well, my grannie is still trying to get me to behave all the time. All of us, as a matter of fact."

"Mom passed her magic to me, well, the two of us. I'm not entirely sure what all that entails at the moment. Because, like you, it's been a lot to go over in the last twenty-four hours. However, you and your family are immortals that much I did want you to know about in the event you didn't get it through our connection. Your grandparents are elderly, I'm to understand, so they don't have to be. But they'll never be hurt or sick again. Even their bodies will be given a boost, and they won't hurt at all, even from the most severe aches they might have." He thanked her for that. "My skin feels like it's crawling over me I'm getting so much magic right now. How do you feel?"

"I've been trying my best not to think about it. However, the strangest part is that I know about the magic I've been given and how to use it. Rules, too, on what I can and can't do with it. Is that something you gave me?" She thought it had been her mind as she didn't know some of the things that her mother had. "I guess I can see that. I have the next couple of days off to rest up. I'd like to use that time to get to know you better. Nothing sexual or untoward, but just getting general information on you. There is a great deal of it in my mind, but it's all in bits and pieces right now. Besides, I think I'd like to get to know you through you. If that's all right."

"I'd like that. However, there is a huge list of things I have to do with the witchcraft that my mother passed to me. Also, I killed the council just before I was to meet up with my mom. I need to figure out what I'm to do about that as well." He asked if he could help. "I'd like that. But we won't be around here while working, at least for now. Mom has...*had* several homes, and one of them, where she did most of her work, is where I need to be. I'd like it if you were to come along with me."

"Will my family still be able to get in touch with me?" She said that so long as they had a link to him, then there wouldn't be a problem. "Good. I'd hate that they might need me and couldn't find me. Also, you should exchange blood with them so they can contact you as well. If you don't mind."

"No, I wouldn't mind that, but if I need them, or you need someone you don't already have a connection with, you only need to reach out to them. As a familiar to my grand witch, you're as powerful as I am. Perhaps more so with you being a shifter bear." He could only nod at that. It was becoming overwhelming to him again. "How about we just go to the house and work from there? It'll be much more relaxing there than here with all this going on, and we'll spend our time getting things squared away between us."

It was settled then. The two of them would work with the things they'd inherited and get to know each other as well. While he didn't know where they were going to be staying, just that it was a home while working, he decided to ask her about packing himself a bag.

"You won't need anything you can't pull out of the air. However, whatever you want to have, it can't be extravagant. Just the necessaries. You already have the ability to change your clothing at will, correct?" He said that he did. "The house that we're going to will be prepared for us both. In that, it will accommodate itself to things we'll need. Toothbrushes, linens and such. There will be under-witches there, too, that will strive to make food for you that we wish to eat as well. But if you need anything else, just ask. I'm sure you've enough knowledge about magic to know the rule in making your life better and about returning to whatever you borrowed from back three times." Frazier told her that he did know that rule.

Having a few days off didn't mean he wouldn't rest with Amelia. Getting the extra magic had zapped both of them badly. Not in pain, not really, but the magic that was working through his body was making him exhausted all the time. Amelia suggested that he drink a great deal of juice and eat fresh fruits and vegetables to battle the fatigue they were both having. Once they were where they were headed, he thought that a good nap would help him out. It was that, or he was going to be falling asleep in his soup.

Laughing, he wondered if he asked for potato cheese soup, would someone make it for him. It was Frazier's go-to quick comfort food. And if there was a loaf of homemade bread to go with it, he'd be as happy as he'd ever been with that. While having no idea why that had popped into his head, now it was all he could think about having.

Telling his family where he was headed, he went with Amelia to the home. They had the power to make themselves come and go as they pleased, but he was thrilled when she suggested that they take his truck to the opening of the house. Like him, he thought that she was overwhelmed too.

He didn't know what he had expected when she said they'd be working from a house that a grand witch owned. It was like a large hotel setting with the most beautiful gardens he'd ever seen. Not picking any of the flowers, he did stop at some of them to smell their strong scents before moving on. Even the trees, full of blooms and fruit, were beautifully maintained and healthy.

As with the witches in the household, plenty were working in the gardens as well. Some of them weren't as young as others, but they all worked well together. He asked her if there was any kind of prison, not having any idea where that thought had come from.

"No. I remember there might have been one centuries ago, but it has long since been abandoned. Even with taking their craft from them when they'd be put behind bars, most of them would be able to escape. Or harm those that were caring for them. After a time of losing more than we were imprisoning, mom did away with it and dealt with their crimes in a quicker way." He asked her if that meant death. "It does. I think because of that, there was less crime. If you have it in your head when you start some shit that if you're caught, you're most assuredly going to die, it keeps most people on the good side of the rules. Not that we don't get an occasional bad witch, but we deal with them the same way."

He was shown around the house by one of the witches. Amelia had to take care of some personal business before she could sit down and talk to him. Frazier was fine with that. Walking about her ancestral home was as much fun as he'd had in a while. Then he came across one of his pieces of art. Amelia joined him near the work just as he was looking for the year on the painting.

"Mom loved to collect art made with natural things. I hadn't any idea this was yours until just now. She was right in saying that you were brilliant. The way you've used what you found in the world to create such a piece makes me think she was also right that you're as one with nature as I am. I pull from the elements as I'm sure you will be able to do now too." He said he used sticks he found in the woods to paint with. And the colors from other things like flowers, moss, and leaves when he needed a certain color. "You'll have to set you up a studio here too. I'm sure you can find yourself plenty of colors here that you might not have on the mountain where you lived."

Frazier was glad that he was shown a bedroom when supper was over for the two of them. He was positive that his head hadn't hit the pillow before he was out. Exhaustion had never taken him under so quickly before in his life.

Chapter 2

"There are other things that have come about that I think need to be looked into. Most of them have to do with the crowding on the mountain pathways and people getting off the actual paths to wander off. I've seen it happen several times since I've been here this week. Or worse yet, fall and hurt themselves. You know as well as I do that it will cause more erosion than you have right now of the mountainsides." Frazier said that he did understand that but wasn't sure that the funding was there to make sure there were more rangers on the paths. "Then you'll have to get more volunteers to come in and work the paths. There isn't any way that this is going to resolve itself. Someone is going to get seriously hurt. Then where will you be?"

Not even bothering answering the question, he asked him how he was working on getting volunteers to work when they were short-staffed already. Kendrick James had been in his office all morning going over the records he'd gathered. Since his brothers were out and about in the field, it had left him in the office. And the only one that could go over the paperwork with him.

"Well, you'll just have to work on that, won't you." He glared at him when Frazier laughed. "What do you think is so funny, Ranger Cross? The fact that you don't think this is a big deal or that I'm assigning you to look for volunteers? We'll need you to recruit about two hundred so that we'll be able to narrow it down to the fifty or so that we need. I've also made up a list of requirements for them to work in the park."

"Have you ever looked at an application for volunteers?" Kendrick asked him why he'd bother with that. "Because it might show you why we don't get hundreds of volunteers coming in daily for a job. One that I might point out to you doesn't offer any kinds of perks like paid vacation time nor retirement money. Coming here to volunteer will get you college credits if you wish to have them, but there isn't any kind of compensation for those who come in on their own time to work. The people will need to be able to hike and carry tools when necessary, which means that they'll be asked to perform strenuous and often time difficult manual labor. Lifting heavy objects is just one of the many duties they might have to perform. Then there is knowing how to use hand tools — rakes, shovels, picks and loopers. Then they have to figure out from about ten pages of jobs they might think they could work at. Also, you might not realize this, but there is no housing for the volunteers that come here to donate their time. How do you think that's going to work out for them?"

"I don't care how you get it done. I just want you to get the people in here." Frazier stood up when Amelia came into the room. Smiling at her, she looked at Kendrick and glared. "Who are you that would be interrupting an important meeting between Ranger Cross and I?"

"This is my future wife, Mr. James, and I would wish that you'd not speak to her in that tone." Kendrick looked at him, then back at Amelia. "He wants me to work to get several hundred volunteers in here to help out with the path erosion issue we have going on. I was just telling him I didn't think that was going to work out so well for him."

"What he's not telling you is that I'm demanding he gets it done. Or I'll have to find someone that will." Amelia asked Kendrick if that usually worked for him, threatening government employees. "I'm not threatening him. Tell her that I'm not threatening you, Cross."

"He's threatening me with something. While he wasn't clear on what he was going to do about getting someone else to do what he wants, it did sound to me like he was making a threat." Kendrick started sputtering around about how he'd taken it the wrong way. "Mr. James, can you tell me who it is that sent you here today? I know for a fact that you don't work for the government. Nor do you work for this park. I know that you think you have some kind of authority over what happens here because you're under the illusion that your taxes pay for this park. They don't. This is completely covered by donations that have been around since before you or I were born."

"You've got that wrong. The money that I pay in taxes comes here, and that's what pays your wages, young man." Frazier simply reached into his drawer and pulled out the book that told how the park had come to be and how it was maintained through donations from large donors. He handed it to him. "Yes, I have this same booklet in my hotel room. It's all wrong. I asked my accountant, and he told me my taxes are used to pay for the roads. This place has roads, doesn't it? Well, that's what I'm paying for. No one can get to the park if I don't pay my taxes. So this is what is going to happen, Ranger Cross. You're going to listen to me and anyone else that comes in this office with ideas on how to keep this place in good working order."

"And we are." Opening the door to his office, Frazier smiled at Mr. James. "I've listened to you, sir, and while I appreciate your input, it's not up to me or you on what is done to do the things you've suggested. I would, however, suggest that you get with the congressman in your state to have him look into things for you. And see how you can make a difference if that's what your plan was when coming here."

"It takes all kinds of red tape to be able to see him.

And it's difficult. So I thought that I'd go right to the source in this and see someone in charge." Frazier told him that he wasn't in charge of the park. "But you're here, running things, aren't you? That's the person that I need to speak to. Who's in charge of this place? I want to speak to them."

"The park is federally owned and managed by the National Park Service. The running of this park is put into their annual budget each year. As for who is in charge of that, you'll have to figure that out on your own." Frazier pointed to the door. "I'm sorry, Mr. James, but I have a lot of things to do today, and I think we're finished here. I hope you enjoy the rest of your stay in the park." After he was gone, still talking about getting more people working here, Frazier closed the door and sat at his desk.

"Do you get many people like him in here?" Frazier told Amelia that they did, but it was his first one. "I bet there are a great many people that think that they have the best idea on how this park needs to be run. This is a great big place. And running it must be a nightmare."

"Not really. We keep on top of things as best we

can. Work through the list of things that need to be done. Hopefully, we don't have any terrible weather or a fire." He grinned at her. "I'm assuming that you got all your work finished for the day."

"No. I got a start on it, but I had a lot of calls coming in about my mom being gone. People trying to figure out what had happened to her. One of the witches asked me if she could take over my mother's job 'to run it correctly.' I just hung up on her and went on with my work. Mom must have known that she was going to be dying because she left me this list of shit that I have to get done right away." She handed him the list. "Some of the things on there have to do with you. She said that you need to be put on my accounts. I had to look that one up and figure it out. I thought she meant like bank accounts, but it's on my witchery account too. I have no idea why you'd need to be on that, but you are now. As well as my banking information."

"What is a witchery account?" She told him. "I had no idea that you might put magic aside to give to others in need. Is this for younger witches or just anyone who might need a boost to their lives?"

"Both. It's money that is used to help a family

that has lost their parents. A student might need some extra cash to buy some expensive books. They might not be witches, but they're related to or good friends to one." He told her that his family did that as well. "Your grandda told me. He said the Cross family has been helping out around the area since before he'd been born. I think that's nice of you guys."

"It wouldn't always be money; you understand that, don't you?" Amelia told him that Grandda had explained that most of the time, it wasn't cash. "No. It might be some wood that they need to warm up their home. A side of meat to help fill some bellies. Grannie would be out in the garden with a couple of young kids, filling up their baskets along with telling them some story about how she just had too much to handle this year. That works better, she told me once, on children than adults." They both laughed.

"My mom did that too, but of course, it was all magical. She'd hear about some husband that was in the hospital, and the family needed a ride to get to see him and back home. Other times they'd win some kind of grocery lottery that would feed them for a few weeks. Stuff like that. She would even send a couple of witches to a house to 'fix' up their washer or dryer if it wasn't working." Frazier thought all of those were good causes and told her that. "Yes, she was very big on keeping those around her happy. She told me that if you could make one person happy in a day, you were doing a great job. I'm lucky if I can make one happy a year. And usually, that's by me going in the opposite direction that they're in."

"Are you going to keep up with those things she did?" Amelia said that she was going to try, but she didn't like people all that much. "You've not met my sister-in-law Sunny yet. She has some anger issues with people. Calls the adults clumps and the children clump-its. She keeps my brother Dexter on his toes most of the time."

"Do you think that I will as well? You, not your brother Dexter." Frazier asked her if she wanted to keep him on his toes. "That's the stupidest answer to a question I've ever heard. Why do men always sound like when you ask them a question, it's part of a conspiracy or something. That it's going to trap them into some kind of commitment."

"Are you going to be this combative all the time?

If so, I might need to wear body armor or something." She told him she was sorry. "It's all right. Just tell me what has you up in arms over a question."

"This morning, I told you I was going to check on some of the things I'd not done yet with my mom's things. I found a notebook about your family. I told you that she said that she had to work with nature to get us mated, right?" He said that she had. "Well, I didn't realize how extensive her notes on your family were. Like I know that your father fell over a fall and that several days later, your mom jumped into the same waterway. She even has notes on when her babies were left in the house alone when she left to follow your father."

"Yes, Grandda told us about that a week or so ago." While he was sure that we didn't want to know, he thought that it couldn't do him much harm in asking. So he did. "What else have you found? I'm sure for as many years we've been on this mountain that there has been a few things that had to be hidden away."

"Not really. At one point, there were ten families living on the land. But as the city life called to them, most of them left. Your grandparents have stayed the longest here because they were born right here on this mountain and have lived out their lives here too." He asked about deaths. "Now, there have been quite a few of those over the years. Unexplained deaths that your grannie might have known about that I can now tell her about. Several people wandered onto the property. Three, as a matter of fact, were killed by the wildlife, and they were left where they lay. Two men and one woman were killed by crashing their getaway vehicle into a tree while evading the police. You and I might go find that one. It's still an open case. Two suicides from cliff jumping—not related to each other. Also, this one isn't deaths, but there was about ten years ago a missing family that has never been found that are still squatting on the land nearest the entrance to the park."

"Grandda knows about them. A family of four, parents and their two kids. They're evading some kind of family trouble. We kept up with it in the newspaper, and that was all it was about that we could find." She said that they could go home now, everything that they were hiding from was now resolved. "I'll tell Grandda. He'll be able to go there and run them off now. I think he's been talking about it for a while now. None of that sounds too serious, does it?"

"Other than the bank robbery, no, not really. There are also things like hunters coming on the land that were shot at to get going. A couple of fishermen, too, that met with some buckshot in their asses. But all in all, not too much going on around with strangers on the land." He asked about other things, such as family. "Nothing there either. Not much, anyway. Your parents would go deep into the woods to fight. My mom came upon them a couple of times when they did that. So you children wouldn't hear. Other marriages, throughout the line, weren't very faithful to each other and met people out in the wooded area as well. I've taken precautions to keep people from coming onto the land to hunt mushrooms. Also, to keep people from using metal detectors as well. Not that big of a deal, but if they were hurt, they might think about suing your family."

"Thank you for that." She said it was her pleasure. "Now that you've helped me out a great deal, what is it I can do for you to help you out? I've been messing around with the magic that you gave me. I can now make a cup of tea and bring it to me mostly without losing any of the hot liquid. I think I've mastered snapping my fingers, but it doesn't seem to work on anything I want to do with it."

They both laughed, and Frazier thought it was a wonderful sound coming from her. As they talked about other things that he'd been working on as well as the paperwork that he'd been filing, he thought he'd had a very productive day.

Occasionally he'd field a call from some of the people visiting the park. Direct some of the people that worked in the park to them if it came to that. He'd also been able to pinpoint a lost child by using the magic he had as well. It ended well for all of them.

"I'm out of here in about an hour. If you want, we can grab dinner on the way home or order something to eat when we get there. I've not had a lot of time to look into getting groceries for the house. Also, getting food delivered isn't possible, sadly. We would have to go and pick up whatever we wanted." She said she was all right with eating before going home. "Good. No clean up."

As they left the park building after his

replacement showed up, they held hands. Or better yet, Amelia reached for his hand, and he held onto her tightly. Once they were in the truck on their way to a restaurant, he realized he'd fallen in love with Amelia. In just the five days they'd been getting to know one another.

~*~

David had never chopped wood in his entire life. If asked a couple of days ago, he thought it was a job he never wanted to do again. But now that he'd been at it for a few days, he was beginning to feel like he wasn't making too many mistakes. Not to mention, he was sleeping much better than he had even before his wife had died. Pausing to have a little look around, he thought about his wife.

Lily had been gone for a month now. It sometimes felt like it was longer. Other times it didn't seem as if anytime had passed. The pain in his heart would hurt so much. But that was getting better too. He wasn't so emotional all the time. While she had committed suicide and he understood some of why she did it, he still missed her more than he had his own parents when they passed away.

She'd been in remission from breast cancer for three years when this latest test had come back that it had spread again. Not only in her lymph nodes but also in her lungs and spine this time. While he did hope that the test would come back negative, he knew deep in his heart that there were signs that it was back to take more of her from him. Then, she'd done the unthinkable. His Lily had killed herself.

"How's it going?" David smiled at Amelia. She frightened him just a little. "You do know that I'd never do anything to harm you, David. You're as much my family as the rest of the Cross family is. Want me to fix your hands? Or I can take away the pain if you'd like."

"Take my pain away? I don't understand." Amelia put out both her hands, palms up. Staring at them for some moments, he finally looked at her. "Could you have? For me, could you have taken her cancer away?"

"Yes. But I wouldn't have been able to keep you both from harm had I done that." David sat down, barely missing the axe in his hand when he did. He put it beside him so he'd not hurt either of them with it. "The way that things went is the way they must be,

David. Her dying, even the way that she did, it is a timeline that all creatures of the earth must follow. Had I known her, or you for that matter, keeping her from having cancer would have had a horrific tumble-down effect that would have been much worse than her dying the way she had."

"I don't understand. You mean that even if you had known her and had been able to make her cancer free, she still would have died. In some other way?" Amelia only nodded. "You said both of us. We both would have died. I think that I would have much preferred that than having to see her with her wrists slit in our bathtub, Amelia. She was all I had."

"No, she wasn't. Otherwise, you'd not be here with your friends." She put out her hands again, and he could see the day that he'd called for Mark and Sunny. His voice was so full of sorrow that he thought that he could die right then. "I can see a bit in the future. My mom could as well. Shall I show you, and this is just one of the many things that could have happened had she not died that morning? And trust me when I tell you, David, this is the least harsh one that I've seen. Remember this, nature needs to have a balance.

You cannot take something away from a line without it having to readjust itself to make things happen the way that it was intended."

He watched as the people on her palm began to change, going back to the time the two of them got up that sad morning. When he was in bed, his alarm went off, and he got up.

"The doctor was supposed to call that morning before I left for work." Amelia told him the doctor had been violently ill all night and had to go to the hospital. He'd only got up long enough from his hospital bed to call Lily and tell her what he'd found. "I didn't know that. I never thought of him having to do anything but ruin our lives."

The changes this time were the good news. He could see it on his wife's face. When she put down the phone, she sat on the side of the bed sobbing. David asked Amelia if the news had come back to her wrong.

"No. She was told that her cancer was completely gone at this time. She doesn't believe the doctor. Thinks perhaps he's giving her false hope. Lily thinks you've convinced him somehow to tell her that it's in remission so that she'll be happy on her last days."

She finally joins him in the dining room. Telling him about the test. "Lily goes on to believe that she's been lied to. No amount of more tests, no letting her see the paperwork will convince her otherwise that she was cancer free. Even me telling her that, proving that I'm strong enough to do it, will change her mind."

The view changed to him and Lily at the doctor's office. Time and time again, if their change of clothing is any indication. It seemed like they were going every day for a month before the narrative stopped. Amelia looked at him.

"You couldn't take it any longer. Your heart was hurting you. The stress of telling her she was fine, taking her to the doctor when she begged you to. Just simply worrying about her endlessly took a toll on you. Then there was your work. You went there no matter the day you'd had with your Lily because it was the only place you could be free of all the things going on at home." The image showed him now, lying in bed with the police over him. "You had a massive stroke in the middle of the night one month after Lily was declared cancer free. Had she been with you, instead of looking things up on the computer that she thought were signs of cancer, she would have seen the pain and agony that you suffered with it."

"You're not blaming her, are you?" Amelia told him that she was only showing him what one of his futures might well have been. "She was afraid. I should have...I don't know what I could have done, but I should have taken better care of myself. I think she might well have been a better person to leave behind. Lily was always so much stronger than I am."

The next thing that he saw was her driving her car. The car, a birthday gift from him the month before she died, was bright red. It seemed to glow in the night with the moon shining on it. The black interior had been embroidered with roses and lilies, her favorite flowers.

Nothing could have prepared him for what happened next. Lily was driving along, listening to music that he could hear when she plowed through a red light, the reflection of it bouncing off the car as trucks and cars slammed into the little red car, tossing it to and fro like it were nothing more than a ball on a pool table.

"Christ, no." He looked at Amelia when the

accident suddenly disappeared. "No. She'd didn't do that. She wouldn't have ended her life, not like that. Please tell me, Amelia, it didn't happen to my lovely Lily."

"I told you, David. Nature needs a way to balance. When she didn't die in the timeline that had been set up for her, she had to die in a different way. A more violent way. You didn't die in the first place, but you did in the second. There are so many more ways that the balance worked through that have you dying in a much worse and painful way." He asked her why she'd shown him that. "Because of this."

Her hands twirled around. The magic of it forming a couple. He couldn't see their faces, but he could see that they were in trouble. When he appeared on the scene, he had his gun out, something that he'd not touched since coming here. David watched as he, in the vision, checked out the couple to make sure that they weren't hurt too badly.

"When you hear the gunshots, I want you to go out the back." He heard the barely whispered order and wondered what was going on. The couple nodded and then stood. The woman, whomever she could have been, was fat with child and holding her belly. "I'll be out in a few minutes. Just run to the van that's out there. Please. If I don't come out right away, you have to leave without me. They're waiting on you."

"Do I die there then?" She told him that he was immortal now. And couldn't die. He watched as he moved along the tall pallets of boxes, careful where he stepped with each movement. The person he seemed to be looking for was standing nearby, his gun at the ready. His face, like the couple, wasn't something he could make out. "That man there, the one in the shadows, who is he?"

"I don't know. I don't know the couple either. They are only one couple that you saved because you came here. Your work with Jamie and Mark is something that you fall into one night when you are asked to help. You become a very important person to a great many people. Because you are here now." He looked at her. David knew that his eyes were full of unshed tears. As they began to roll down his cheeks, he asked her if she was telling him something that he needed to hear or if this was the truth. "I cannot lie to you, David. None of us can because we all consider you family. And I would hope that you know me well enough to know that I wouldn't anyway. You're a good man. A better friend to everyone here than you think you are. You are a thriving part of this family and someone that we've all come to love and trust. This, right here, is your future. But only if you want it."

"You could take this all away." She nodded. "I don't think I want to know how you do it, but I believe you."

He sat there for a long time, not really thinking about anything. His mind seemed to be blank. When she put out her hands again, as she had done when she had first joined him, he asked her what would happen if she were to take the pain away.

"You would lose a hand from a splinter that you can't feel." He stared at her for a second before laughing. "You find it funny that you would die so stupidly?"

"No. I find it funny that you said that just like you were telling me about the weather. And if you take the blisters away, what will happen then?" She told him. "I would be able to chop more wood so that this winter, none of us freeze. I don't believe I've ever had calluses before. I think perhaps I'd go with those rather than losing my hand."

She brought his hands into hers and kissed the back of them. When she released them, standing as she did so, he wondered at someone so confident in themselves that they could just give you the information that she thought you'd need and then walk away. He asked her what she was going to do now.

"We're going on a hike to find a car that was used in a bank robbery." He laughed again. "Would you like to join us, David? It's about an eight-mile hike up the mountainside."

"No thanks. I think I'd rather stay here and chop wood on level ground. At least here, I know that I won't run into any bears." She was still laughing when Frazier came out of the house and took her hand into his. As they walked into the tree line and out of his sight, he thought about what he'd said. He supposed being afraid of bears when he lived with a sleuth of them was sort of silly. David bent to his task, trying his best not to think of what if and why's for a change.

Though he had to admit he did feel calmer than he had. Also, his hands, while still a little sore, weren't nearly as painful as they had been before his talk with Amelia. David thought that he might be on the road to recovery. He hoped so anyway.

Chapter 3

The walk was wonderful, Frazier thought. There was just enough crispness in the air that he could tell that soon, the mountain tops would be covered deeply in snow. When Amelia asked if they could stop for a moment, he did so without hesitation. The two of them had been enjoying their last couple of days together, and he was thrilled beyond words that he belonged to her.

It had been two weeks since the two of them had found each other. And he couldn't have been more in love with her than he was right at this moment. Yesterday she'd taken him, by magic, to each of the homes they both owned since her mom had died. Amelia was looking for a spell book that had belonged to her mother and couldn't find it among her things. As of this morning, it was still missing.

"How often do you guys hike up here?" Frazier told her he couldn't remember the last time he'd been in this direction. "Yes, well, it does look untouched, doesn't it. Like it was just waiting for the two of us to come along and discover something. Besides the car, I mean."

"That's what I feel like every time I go on a tour with people at work. Here too, but it's more profound for me when I have a group of people with me. They'll see something, or I will, and I have to refrain myself from going on and on about whatever it is for hours. We don't have that much time for me to be too wowed over a salamander or a bug." She laughed, and he loved that part about her too. She was never too serious for him. "I have been known for going overboard on information when talking to people."

She laughed again. It was unrestrained yet beautiful too. "The view from here is spectacular, don't you think? I mean, you can see for miles and miles, and I'm betting that if I were to venture a little forward, I'd see things below me that are just as amazing." She moved closer to the edge of the slip they were on. "I was thinking about this place last night. Not here but nearer the edge of your mountain. How lovely — and dangerous — it would be to have a house sitting so close that you only had to go out your back porch to see all the wonders of this park. I love it here."

"I do as well. I can't imagine living anywhere else." She agreed with him. "My father loved to take long walks. I think now that I know better that it was to get us boys out of the house for my mom. Grandda told us that she was never happy living here."

"That's sad. I feel sorry for her that she didn't get to love all that was around her." Frazier told her that he was sorry as well. "I wonder if she would have ever come to enjoy being here with you boys had she not died. I believe that it would certainly have been different for you boys if she had stayed to raise you. Don't you agree?"

"I don't think that any of us would have been able to stay here. I don't know why, but I think, being our mother, she would have taken us at some point to a larger area that had no mountains around it. Certainly not Tennessee. She would have wanted flat places and city lights. Not that it matters too much now, I suppose. I hate to think about what brought her to her decision, but I've come to think she was quite selfish in doing what she had. Just leaving us in the house without a thought as to if we'd be all right there. That's what she did the day she leaped off the waterfall to kill herself." Amelia told him she was sorry that she'd brought it up. She'd not meant to hurt him. "No, it's not your fault. My brothers and I have been talking at different times over the months about the stories that Grandda and Grannie would tell us about the two of them. Mother was selfish in that she made my father's life difficult because she hated it here so much. I would have figured that she should have known about the law stating that we'd have to live here in order to keep the land. But we'll never know that."

"I couldn't imagine bearing six children and then leaving them in a house alone to do what she did. I suppose you should be grateful that she didn't do any harm to the six of you. That seems to be the trend. People killing off their children rather than having to deal with them anymore." Frazier held Amelia in his arms while she spoke. "I know that not every person goes to those extremes. I know that. But you read about it more and more in the newspaper. I'm so happy that she didn't harm any of you. Maybe—perhaps she wasn't as selfish as she could have been. Also, she provided for the six of you, too, so that you'd be able to support yourselves as well."

"Yes. They both did that for us." He stood there holding her while he watched the clouds, fluffy white ones, dance over the mountains and trees. Off in the distance, he could hear the screech of a hawk. The bellow of some cross animal. When Amelia told him she was ready to go, he kept her hand in his, and they started up the mountain once again.

Just after two, they reached the car. He was surprised to see that it seemed to be in good shape for as old as it was. It had been in the thirties when it had disappeared. It looked to him as if, other than the rust all over it, nothing had bothered it since it came to rest against the tree.

"Look how the growth of the tree pulled up the front of it. Almost as if it was a jack so that someone could look under the hood." Walking around it, he could see the tires had been long since rotted. Pieces of them were missing that he was sure could be found in a den somewhere. He wiped at the window in the back seat and could just make out a skeleton of one of the occupants there. "I can see one person in here. How many do you think will be found?"

"Three people. A woman and two men." She told him their names. "Clara would have been twenty-five at the time of their deaths. The man, brothers were seventeen and twenty. Some speculate that she was the ring leader, but she wasn't. Tommy, the youngest, was."

"Sort of like Bonny and Clyde, I guess." She told him that was what she'd been thinking. "There are some bullet holes back here in the trunk. I guess I'm assuming that's what they are. I guess we should open the doors and see what we can find out."

"Can you do that?" He told her that he was a federal officer. "Oh. I guess I forgot that you'd have the authority to do that. If you want to wait to open it, I know exactly what you're going to find. If you wanted, you more than likely know as well. But I think it would be more fun just to open it up—not that I'm morbid, but this case is so old that it's something you don't run across every day."

It took him longer than he thought it should to get the driver's side door open. He didn't want to rip it off the body of the car, but it had been closed longer than he'd been around. Getting it open, he was shocked to see that the three bodies were intact. Other than they were dead, of course.

"It looks like maybe rats or other small rodents were able to get inside and tear at the clothing. I don't want to think about what else might have gotten to their bodies." Frazier surmised they were in good shape because the windows had been closed, and nothing could have breached the doors. "I guess that's good. What do we do now? I mean, other than stay with it until someone comes to look it over."

"I need to call it in. Find a place that I'm sure they'll want a helicopter to be landed nearby." Amelia pulled out what she thought was the bank bag and looked inside. "Money?"

"Yes. It's old too. It's sad to think that they went through all this only to end up being killed by crashing their car into a tree." He showed her that Tommy had been shot in the back of his head. More than likely from a bullet coming up from the trunk when he was hiding in the back seat. Clara had been shot in her chest. Frazier thought it had come up the same way and caught her in mid-chest. Their bones showed that much to them, at least. "So these two died by the police, and poor old George died by the car crashing. I wonder what his last thought was when the tree popped up in front of him."

"Probably 'well fuck a duck and watch it waddle.' George might not have known that the other two were dead before that. Or they might not have been yet." They were enjoying making up stories about how they'd died and come to be on their mountain. It was morbid, sure, but they'd had nothing to do with them dying.

He made the call to the main office of the park first, then to the police. It was Mark, who was running the desk today, that suggested that he contact someone in their office. Just to make sure that everyone who might want to be involved was informed. Not that he thought it would go quietly in the night. This was going to be big news for everyone.

It turned out to be a shit show. Every time someone new came on the scene, he was questioned about how they'd found the car. It was getting to the point that he wished that the two of them hadn't gone looking for the car. It wasn't until David showed up with food for him and Amelia that he felt like he had someone there that he could lean on.

"I heard it on the news that the car had been found with bodies in it about two hours ago. Just as your grannie was making your lunch for you, they were able to contact some of the relatives of the deceased. To think that after all this time, there is someone out there related to them still. Apparently, Clara had a husband and child that she had left behind. He has kids of his own now and has barricaded himself in his house." Amelia said that was what she'd more than likely do too. "Yes, he has about twenty news vans in his yard, all of them with cameras and phones pointed to his front door. It looks to me like he could have used the money for this. By the way, did you know there was a reward for finding this car and the money?"

"I've been told that there is several times by the public, the police, as well as the coroner that had to come all the way up here to pronounce that the three skeletons in the car were dead." The three of them laughed. "But in all seriousness, no, I didn't even think about that when we came out here to find the car. It was just a way for us to get out and about to talk to each other."

It was well after dark when they were headed home. He had better eyesight than any of the people with them, so he led the way down. Amelia held onto David to keep him from tumbling down the hill, and he watched over his grandda, who had decided that it was too much going on for him not to be somehow involved. It was fun for them all, Frazier thought. Especially his grandda who remembered when the robbery had taken place.

"I'd only been a wee bit of a boy at the time, but I remember it. Everyone was speculating on where they might have gone off to and what they were spending their ill-gotten gains on. My daddy thought they'd gone all the way to Middlesboro, Kentucky. I remember thinking that it was a fer piece to be going in a car, but it would only take a person a couple of hours to get there nowadays." Grandda laughed. "Of course, cars didn't travel all that fast or well back then, I don't think."

Grannie had a few things to say about it as well, even going so far as to drag out old albums with the newspaper clippings stuck in them. She told them how her mom had saved them so that when the car was found, she could compare the notes of what people had been saying back then about where the people had ended up.

"I don't think anyone ever wanted to believe they all died. It was, for lack of a better way to say it, romantic to all of us kids. They robbed a bank, and back then, we all thought they'd gotten away with it. Were out spending the money on things like movie pictures and the such." She laughed a little. "Tommy was such a good-looking kid. My older sister, she would look at the pictures of him and just sigh like she'd been his one and only love. Silly girl. I wonder what she might have thought if she'd known he was only a hop up the hill dead in his car."

That night when they were sitting around the living room, Amelia asked his grandparents if they had ever planned to leave the mountain when they'd been younger. All six of their grandsons just stared at them, waiting, like he was on their answer. They looked at each other before answering.

"No. Not once. I met your grannie when she was just a baby, it seems like now. She was all of fifteen, and I was a strapping sixteen-year-old. Both of us had us a good job. My daddy, he worked in the park then, and he worked hard. He'd bring me into town with him every day so that I could work for a couple of little places around that needed an extra hand or two when there were people traveling in." Grandda looked at Grannie, and Frazier was shocked at the look of pure love they had for each other, even after all these years. "Your grannie, she worked in one of the ladies shops in town. They sold some of them fancy hats that women liked to wear back then. I was bringing home about a dollar or two a week. Your grannie, she was bringing home a bit more as she worked longer hours. But it did help me ask her out on a date."

Grandda told stories of him courting grannie. How their wedding had been pulled off and the house that had been built for them when they had their daddy. By the time he was telling of dad meeting their mom, the story had been wonderfully whimsical. Like something you'd read or see in a black and white movie. Only it was his family they were talking about, and it was nice to have such memories told to them.

~*~

Amelia looked out the window of the room she'd been staying in. It was sometimes difficult to remember that she wasn't in the times of when Frazier's grandparents had been born. Nothing about the scene she was watching had her thinking of the city far beyond here, filled with people traveling up and down the road in their loud cars and avoiding running down pedestrians that thought they were above being hit by a car while in the town.

Below her were four big bears. All of them were shifters and Cross bears. They were wrestling around, like children after a rainstorm in the mud and grass. The other two, she thought it to be Mark and the youngest Ewing — it was difficult to tell in the darkness — sitting as their other selves on the sidelines watching. Ewing would be leaving in the morning to go to a zoo on the other side of the country to take two bear cubs as well as a couple of mountain lion cubs that had been orphaned when the hill slide had happened a month ago.

"You'd think he was going to be gone for a year the way they're acting out there." Sunny sat beside her on the window seat. Jamie joined them a few minutes later with a bottle of wine that grandda had made last fall. She poured them all a glass. "I love this stuff. It's so sweet you forget that it could be dangerous for you after a couple of glasses of it."

They didn't talk much but sipped their drink and watched the antics below them. It wasn't until they either got bored or just tired that they sat back in their seats that Amelia told them what she'd been holding from them for the past few days.

"I have some things that I'd like to give the two of you. It's a gift from my mom. There are similar ones for the other brides that come to be here as well. It's magic, so I don't know what it will give you or do to you, but you'll be able to figure that out when the time comes. It comes with instructions on how to use it as well as what it does. Like the magic that Frazier and I got, it sort of downloads with the magic." Sunny asked if it was something that she'd need to share with her mate. "No. She said that it was just for the women. I'm not sure, but I think it has something to do with labor and delivery when you have your babies. But don't hold me to that. It's just the first thing that popped into my head when I found the box." She put out her hand, and the magic simply went to them. Amelia turned to the window again before continuing. "I'd been searching for my mother's spell book for the last several days. I don't know why I didn't ask someone at her house where it was. I guess I thought it would be a well-kept secret by a witch of grandeur. Turns out it was on the bookshelf with the rest of her books in the kitchen. No spell books there but cookbooks that, for some reason, she collected over the years. I never once saw her cooking even popcorn while I was living at home."

She knew they were confused, so she laughed a little before telling them why she'd even mentioned it. Amelia told them about the spell she'd been looking for that would make it so that her magic would take care of the family even if they left the mountain.

"I don't think any of the family has it in their head that they're going to leave. But you might know something that we don't. Do you?" She didn't answer Sunny but sat staring out the window. "Now I'll have to think about that for a long time until all of Cross's have mates like we do. Come on, tell us what you're thinking."

"I can't. I won't either. It's just bits and pieces of the future that I can see. In much more detail than when my mom could do it, I think. Anyway, it's not that I don't want to tell you, but it's just that I can't. I don't know enough at this point to even tell you who it might well be. It could be the grandparents leaving the mountain by death. I just don't know." They both thought that was a good enough answer and let it go. "Tomorrow, I have to have a meeting with a group of witches that have been going beyond the boundaries that they should be. They've been doing things that are against our bylaws, and I'm going to have to either kill the lot of them or figure out another way to have them punished. Death is the only thing that I think will stop them."

"You don't sound all the happy about it either way. Is it dark magic?" She told Sunny that it was. "I've dealt with that sort of magic before. Not often, but enough to know that it's dangerous to those that use it and those that are targets of it. I've also had to deal with other creatures while working for the government. It's a little scary to know that for whatever people think about things that go bump in the night, they're much more frightening than they think."

"I agree with you there." Amelia finally turned from the window before speaking again. "These witches that I have to go and see are, for the most part, young witches that have been caught up in things that they should have left alone. But now, with the ones in charge, four older, like as old as the grandparents older, have taken the dark magic to a level that is beyond anything that I've had to deal with before. But then, I've never been the grand witch until recently."

"Are you afraid?" Amelia said that she was more afraid of the unknown than the women. "I guess I can see that. I can go with you if you'd like. I have this knack for being able to find people before they find me. Would that help you? Also, since all this magic is coming to us, I've also figured out that I'm a good deal stronger than I used to be at a lot of things. Like reading people's minds."

"I think that I'll be all right." She glanced out the window before speaking. "We've, Frazier and I have been in this house together for an entire month, and he sleeps in the bedroom down the hall. How do I get him into my bed? I mean, I've done everything but come right out and tell him I want a piece of him."

"You have to do that." Amelia asked Jamie what she meant. "You have to tell him that you want a piece of him. It's the only way that it works for these guys. I'm sure he told you when you were first together that he'd only touch you if you came to him or told him. Something like that?" She nodded. "They mean it. You have to—even then, he's going to ask you several times if you're sure before he'll take you to bed. They're great in bed too. I don't know if it's them being bears or what, but they can make you scream and then think they've killed you every time they touch you."

"Seriously?" Jamie nodded then so did Sunny. "But in order to get this wonderful lovemaking, I have to near rape him, and even then, I have to tell him several times that I want him. That's sort of—"

"Yeah, fun." Sunny laughed. "It's also kind of sexy too. To them, you're already his wife. I mean, it's their whole culture with being shifters and finding their mates. I love it. If it hasn't been done already, the paperwork for you two to legally be married is already in the courthouse. I guess they have people in places there that can get things done up like that so that people won't question whether or not you're married when the kids come along. Do you want any?"

"I do." Sunny told her she'd have to tell him when she wanted them too. "Why is that? I mean, does he expect me to raise a child we have on my own, so he wants me to be prepared? That's not going to happen."

"No. Like his brothers, Frazier will say that it's your body, your decision. And I love that. But if you wanted to go back to working, which I'm assuming that you will, he'll gladly be a stay-at-home dad and do all the things that are there for you and the child." Amelia needed to think about that and told her so. "They're the best men in the world as far as I can see. None of them would harm you—in fact, any one of them would die for you. Not that they can, thanks to you, but it is something that they'd of done before you gave us all immortality. I'm not kidding, Amelia. There aren't more romantic, wonderfully kind men in the world but for the men in this family."

After they left her to go back to their own rooms, she noticed that the men were all sitting around a fire talking. She didn't want to go down there and make him come to bed with her, so she found herself a tee shirt and made her way to his room. This shit was for the birds.

It wasn't hard to find the room that he'd been using. It was so far away from the master bedroom she'd been using that she thought of using breadcrumbs to get her back if he sent her packing. Getting into his bed, she could tell he wasn't cold at night because there was only a sheet on the bed and a lighter quilt than the one she had on her bed. Snuggling down into the cover, she would swear it took her nearly ten minutes to get warm enough to stop shivering.

The house was quiet on this end of it. Her room, the one she'd been using, was where the barns were, as well as the other homes. Once her eyes adjusted to the room's overall darkness, she realized that it was as dark as a windowless room. Amelia loved that the room was dark. Not a single light came through the windows, as the pine trees were just dense enough to keep the moon out as well.

The pillows that she was using were feather. She only got stuck by a quill once in the cheek before she finally got them to go in one direction and not all willy-nilly. As her eyes drooped more and more, she tried to stay awake so that she could talk to Frazier when he came to bed. But it seemed the more she fought the sleepiness that came over her, the harder it was for her to keep away.

Telling herself that she'd just close her eyes for a moment wasn't going to work either, but she did it. Just a moment, she kept telling herself. It would only be for a moment. Then she'd be better at staying awake for him. They needed to talk, and she wasn't going to be able to do that if she was sound asleep when he finally got his ass in bed.

Chapter 4

Frazier woke up with Amelia wrapped around him. He was aching with the need to get up and go to the bathroom. And hard as stone to boot. Sliding out from under her was proving to be harder than anything that he'd tried before, and he was just ready to give up when she turned and glared at him.

"What are you doing?" He told her that he had to use the bathroom. "It's still dark outside. Did you just get into bed and decide that you had to pee right now? Shouldn't you have taken care of that before coming to bed? Lie still. I'm exhausted."

She rolled over and off him. Getting up as quietly as he could, he heard her growl and him. For some reason, he found that to be as funny as any of the dirty jokes that Mark was telling them last night. Closing the door to the bathroom, he did his business and returned to the bedroom but not before turning off the light.

"I swear to god I'm going to sleep at the other end of the house if you're going to be this inconsiderate every night." She flipped the covers up and told him to get in. "And see if you can lie still for ten minutes before you start doing a rodeo again. Good heavens, I think you're worse to sleep with than my mother when I was little."

Getting into bed, wide awake now, he wrapped what he knew to be his cold body around her. Her squeal of anger had him busting out laughing. Trying to pull her back to him, just so he could warm up his feet on her legs, had her fighting him. Frazier was having so much fun that he couldn't help but point out that it had been his bed she'd invaded, and she would have to suffer the consequences of his cold feet.

He didn't know how long they wrestled around on the bed, but when he ended up on the floor with Amelia on top of him, he pulled her mouth to his and kissed her. It was the first time that he'd been this close to her, and he hoped that it wasn't the last. Rolling her to her back, he slid his hands up her arms and held her hands well above her head.

"I hope you don't have plans for the day." She said that she could easily break them. "Good. Because now that I've got you here, there isn't any way that I'm going to allow you to go back to the other bed and leave me here all alone again."

"I do have to go and talk to some witches. That's important but not until later. Much later. Are you going to kiss me again?" He did. Showing her with his mouth how much he wanted her. "I was beginning to think that you didn't want me. I asked the others, and they said that I'd have to show you that I wanted you."

"You did that in a wonderful way, my dear." He moved over her, adjusting his body so that it fit comfortably over hers. "You fit me nicely, I think. The way my cock seems to know just where to go is nice as well, don't you think?"

"I do, but I think it would fit you better if you were inside of me." Putting both her hands into his one, he tore the top of her gown from her. Taking her hard nipple into his mouth, he suckled it until he decided to taste the other one. "Frazier, you're not getting anywhere as fast as I want you to be."

"I think you just need to calm down and let me enjoy myself. I've dreamed of nothing but having you since I found you. Now I need my fun time." He took the other breast into his mouth and nipped gently at her entire breast before taking the other one into his mouth. Taking his time, he let go of her hands and ran both of his down her body to where her bottom was on the floor. "There are so many times when I had to take several cold showers before I raced down the hall to where you are. And had I known the lovely parts of you that you hid so well from me, I might well have just breached your bedroom and taken you anyway."

"I wish you had. So many times." She moaned, and he joined her. "Oh, Frazier, I love you so much. Please, make me yours."

"I will love. In time. I love you too." He nipped his way down her body to her breastbone. There he feasted on the flesh that made a small indent on her flesh. Moving downward, closer to where he wanted to be, Frazier tore at the rest of her clothing until Amelia was as naked as he was.

Her hips seemed to call to him. Licking them,

then nibbling on them, had her squirming beneath him. Frazier moved to her thigh, then her knees. Tasting her calves as he made his way back up her leg, he could see how wet she was. The floor beneath her was stained with her cream.

Running his fingers from her gate to her clit, he closed his mouth over her and fucked her with his tongue. All the while, he slid his finger in and out of her while drinking down her juices.

Her pussy was warm, and her juices were hot. The more he took from her, the more he wanted. Each time she came for him, small hard to the body little climaxes, Frazier would lap at her clit until she came a second, then a third time for him. Still, he thought, it wasn't enough. He needed her all.

Her hands tangled in his hair. Pulling him upward a little at a time, he was at her navel this time when he paused to play with the well there. Moving up her again, after enjoying such treats as her moans and her begging him for more, he took both her breasts into his palms and suckled them one at a time, nipping at the peaks.

His cock was so close to her pussy that he

could feel her juices as they touched him. Sliding upward, moving his hips in just the way he needed, Frazier moved just the tip of his cock head into her. A powerful climax took her, nearly unseating him as she moved her hips up to take more of him inside of her. When Amelia came again, Frazier slammed forward and felt her tighten around him so tightly that he felt slightly strangled within her. He wasn't sure whether he wanted her to move or not. It was just too much and not enough at the same time. Christ, he loved this woman.

He moved when she did, taking her harder than he had wanted but needing to empty himself deep inside her. Holding her to him, cupping her ass tightly so that he could be as deep as he could, Frazier nuzzled her neck and was thrilled beyond words when she gave her throat to him.

Mine whispered through his mind. *Mine* was all he could think about when he bit down on her pounding pulse. Emptying in her again as his mouth filled with her tangy hot blood, he felt his balls being squeezed for every drop of his cum. He cried out, his bear screaming with him as it felt as if both of them were claiming their mate for all time.

He must have blacked out for a moment, perhaps longer. He wasn't alone on the floor, but he was tangled up in the sheet. Amelia was wrapped quite nicely, he thought, in the blanket and staring at him. Asking her what he'd done, Frazier sat up and wrapped the sheet around him better.

"Nothing. You snore. Loudly too." He grinned at her, and she smiled back. "Of all the things that had been running through my head while I watched you sleep, that isn't anything I was thinking of telling you. I love you, Frazier."

"Oh, Amelia, I love you so very much." He scooted over toward her and nearly killed himself when the sheet got tangled up again around the foot of the bed. "Not the most graceful way of getting a good morning kiss, is it?"

After kissing her, he pulled her closer to him. After sitting there for a few minutes, he finally asked her how long she had before her meeting with the witches. Apparently, she'd forgotten about it because she jumped up, knocking his chin with her head, and then he fell back on the floor again. Bumping his head pretty hard.

Getting into the shower with her, he didn't even bother trying to hide the fact that he was teasing her. She was so angry at him when she was finished washing her hair that she got out of the stall, slammed the door on his toe and made it bleed. It was no less than he deserved, but Christ, he was having the time of his life.

Frazier was just finishing up making the bed when she came into the bedroom with him. As she stood in the doorway, he tried to judge her mood before talking again. When she suddenly burst into tears, he limped to her and held her in his arms, telling her how sorry he was.

"It's all me. Why am I in such a terrible mood?" Not answering seemed to be the best answer of all, he thought. "I don't know what's wrong with me. I feel overwhelmed one minute, and the next, I'm feeling sorry for myself. Tell me it's something that I can fix."

"I have no idea if you can or not, honey." She smacked him on the chest. "You're very violent, aren't you? I've only known you for just a fraction of the time you've been around, and I'm trying to figure you out too. I know that I tease you a great deal. You're so cute when you get all pissy with me. Maybe I'm a sadist or something. I don't know. But I do love you, and if I can help you with whatever has you upset all the time, you tell me. I'm there for you. Could it be this meeting today? Or the people that you're supposed to meet there? Since I don't know a great deal about witchcraft, I can only assume that's what it is."

"I might have to kill them." Asking her if she thought that was what it would come to, he pulled a shirt over his head. "I don't know. I think I've had myself convinced they needed to die from the start of knowing what they're doing, and I can't shake that feeling. Maybe they're nice people who have been judged poorly."

"Do you believe that?" Amelia told him that she didn't think she did. "Yeah, I don't either. Black magic, you said that was what they're using, right? Well, the words black magic makes me think, even not knowing anything, that it's not the right kind to be using on others. Also, if I remember correctly, you said that they were building up their store of magic to take over the coven. Which coven are they trying to take?"

"Mine. Which is stupid because I'm the ruler of all covens, no matter the kind of magic that they use in it." Frazier asked her if there was a protocol book around that he could read. "Yes. There are several, as a matter of fact. Why?"

"I could read up on the rules that govern covens and help you with knowing the laws that you can quote to them. I wanted to be an attorney when I was younger. Grannie said I'd never cut it because I like to have too much fun with people to be too serious. But with this, I think I could help you." She pulled a book out of the air and handed it to him. "That was awesome. Can I do that too?"

"Think of something that you need and put out your hand. You really don't have to put out your hand for it to come to you. It'll just as easily land on the table if you're near one or just appear somewhere close — what are you doing now?" He told her. Amelia opened and closed her mouth three times before finally shrugging. "I started to tell you that won't work, but only because I never thought of doing it before. Do you think that if you hold the book over a table and ask it for rules over black magic, it'll find it? It's worth a try, I think."

He put the book on the nightstand and laid his hand over it. After asking himself what he was looking for, he moved his hand, and the book opened up to the front cover. Then as they both watched, pages began to flip quickly until suddenly, it simply stopped. He read the name of the chapter twice before looking at Amelia

"The rules and regulations of Black Magic." He laid his hand over the chapter again and asked for the bylaws pertaining to taking the coven from the grand witch. Again he moved his hand and watched as the pages flipped. When it stopped this time, he picked up the book. "It says here that they have to not only be stronger than you are, which I don't see happening, but they cannot all charge you at once. One member of their coven has to pick a leader that will match magic to magic with you."

"What does it say about black magic and trying to take my coven?" Reading down the pages until he came to the part where it talked about black magic versus white or even gray magic. "What's gray magic?"

"It's magic that comes from a Black Magic coven that must be taken by the grand witch and then turned into gray. It will become white over time so long as the witch in charge doesn't use any other magic than the pure white of their kind." He looked up at her before reading further down the page. "It says here that you have to warn the coven of any color three times that you're the grand witch—if that is your title—before you kill them. It also says here that there must be at least one death to a black coven before you turn your back on them. Like cutting the head from an asp that is set on killing you."

"Well, that certainly clears things up, doesn't it. I mean, I have to kill at least one of them to follow the rules." She sat down. "Can you really come with me? And bring that book? I might need you to spout off some more rules if they get out of hand. Which, according to my mom's notes, they have several times over the centuries."

"Of course, I'll go with you. What do I have to do? I mean, you said that I was your familiar. So does that mean I get to be my gnarly bear for you?" Frazier pretended to claw out at her, and she finally smiled. "There's what I've been looking for. That beautiful smile of yours. I love you, Amelia, and it would be my greatest pleasure to go with you and kick some black magic butts."

~*~

Now that they were here together, she didn't think it was such a good idea to have brought Frazier. She didn't know what she'd do with herself if something were to have happened to him. And it might. The women that she was here to disband and more than likely kill were a good deal stronger than she had first thought. She looked at Frazier when he cleared his throat.

"They've compiled their magic with hers. They can't do that. I can, as your second in command, put it back where it belongs, but I'd like to have your permission to be your second in command while we're here. Everywhere else, you can be fully in charge." She asked him if she could be in charge in bed. While he pretended to think about it, she gave him permission to be her second. "Putting you in charge in the bedroom might make us miss out on some pretty heady climaxes, but I'll concede that you've been around longer than me and might be better all the way around with sex than I am. How about we put that on the back burner for now."

Again, he made her laugh. All afternoon, while

he read up on the rules of the book, he'd been doing the same thing. Bringing her out of her head so that she wasn't afraid. Because she didn't like that her first official duty as the grand witch was to kill a bunch of wannabes.

He snapped his fingers, and she saw the moment that the magic that had been with the woman in front of her be taken away. She staggered for a bit before she glared at her. It was then that Frazier spoke up. She loved this man.

"You can't do that. As you're well aware. Putting all your magic into one person is against all rules for the magic. However, if you would like to keep the magic that they shared with you, when the grand witch, this woman here, wins, you all will be killed. Up to you." They conferred, and Frazier told her that he could tell somehow that their magic, even all of it in one person, wasn't even half of what she had. Amelia wasn't sure if he could tell that or not, but it did make her feel better. "Once you have decided, it will be so. There will be no turning back once the grand witch here has spoken." Frazier winked at her. "That's twice they've been told."

Bursting out laughing again, she had to clear

her throat before she could stop the laughter burbling from her lips. He'd done it without making it sound like such a big deal. It would count too. As she'd taken him on as her second, then his words were as bonding as her own were.

"We're going to make it, so I have all the magic." One of the women in the back started to back away. "Deedee, if you leave this room, you'll never make it home to that husband of yours. I told you when I brought you here that you were going to be helping us tonight."

"I don't want to be here at all. I've never wanted to be here. I thought this was a book review meeting when you made me come with you. I want no part of any of this." Amelia reached out to Deedee and found that she truly didn't want to be there. That Sandra, her mother-in-law, had made her attend the meetings all these years because she'd lent them enough money to put on their home. "Please, Sandra, please let me go. I won't help you if you—"

"I give you safe passage, Deedee Marks. However, if you turn to black magic again, for any reason, I will kill you without hesitation. Do you understand what

I'm telling you, as I am the grand witch of witches?" Amelia winked at Frazier, telling him that it had been three times now. "If you agree, Deedee, then you are to go home to your husband and children." She was out the door before Amelia was finished speaking. "Is there anyone else here against their will?"

Four other women raised their hands and pledged themselves to her. Amelia made sure that they understood that they were talking to the grand witch, just to be sure, and they said they knew what they were doing. When they left, that left Sandra with only eight more members of her coven.

"You need thirteen to be a coven, Sandra. Surely you knew that." Sandra laughed and said that she'd not had so many rules given to her since she'd been a little kid. "Be that as it may, you're short five members. You can disband or carry on to your death. It's entirely up to you at this point. But I will not hold back because you were stupid enough to start this war."

"I've never been so ready to take you on than I am at this moment." Magic in the form of a black light was tossed at her. Amelia didn't move as it petered out long before it reached her across the room. "That was to show you what you're up against. Your mother knew better than to mess with me and my coven."

"She did. She thought it would have been a waste of her time to have come here and killed you when you can't even hold your coven together. But when you started to kill off lesser witches, it opened up a whole new set of rules that I'm going to make you responsible for. How do you wish to die?" Sandra asked her why she was so sure that she was going to die and not her. "Haven't you been listening to me? I'm the grand witch with the powers not only of my own but those of my mother."

Reaching up into the air, she pulled lightning to her, a tornado, as well as a great ice storm. It was working up to be quite the storm of storms when Frazier shifted into his bear and stood on his back paws. Then the magic of the two of them doubled then tripled before she released it on Sandra and her standing coven.

The screams were cut off. She couldn't see what damage she'd done to the women, but she knew from the smell of blood that some of them were hurt badly, if not dead. When the smoke cleared, she made her way to where the standoff had started and looked at the only woman left. She was so mangled, barely alive, that it made her slightly sick that she'd done this to her.

"You shouldn't have been able to beat me. I'm much stronger than you." Amelia didn't bother with a response. It was obvious who was the stronger of them. "You broke the rules. You should have made me quit."

"I gave you ample opportunity to walk away, Sandra. You're the one that chose to stand your ground. And for what? You're dead, as is your so-called coven is."

"Repair me. I want to be able to come back for you over again." Frazier told her that she was too far gone for that. "You're a shifter. How is that possible that you were able to help her with her magic."

"I'm her mate, and I didn't help her with her magic. I reined it in so that she'd not destroy the earth behind you. I helped control it, not enhance it. All the magic that came at you, it was all her, grand witch Amelia Cross." She leaned back on him when she stood up. Amelia was suddenly exhausted. When a glass of juice was handed to her, she could have jumped for joy that she had a mate like this one. Frazier was perfect.

Exactly what she needed in her life. "I'll clean this up, then we'll go home. All right?"

It took them together only a few minutes to get the bodies cleaned up. The scorched earth would take a while to heal, but it would once she gave it a bit of herself. The women's bodies would be found in a few days. A fire in the building caused by a candle falling over would be blamed for their deaths. The people in town already thought that the group was off their rocker, so this wouldn't be a surprise to any of them that this came about.

Once they were home again, she helped Frazier move his things back to the master bedroom. Once things were just how they wanted them, everything was put away and neatly stacked, they headed to the kitchen for dinner. One of the women in the group that had left was standing there waiting for them.

"I would wish to serve you, my lady, my lord." She nearly told the woman, Tabby, that she didn't want her around her, but Frazier asked her what her qualifications were. "I can cook and clean. I'd rather cook if you'd not mind, but I can clean too. I want to repay you for my life and that of my daughter. Sandra, well, I don't like speaking ill of the dead, but she blackmailed us into following her, and we couldn't get free. It's been more decades than I like to think about, and since then, Patty and I have outlived our families and have no one else to put up with us anymore."

"Is Patty going to be working for us too?" The timid little woman came out of the pantry with her arms loaded up with things that she didn't think had been in there before. "You'll follow the rules of the white magic, correct? You'll never bring the dark or gray into this house, or you will be killed. I won't cut you any slack even if you make the world's greatest apple pie. I will gut you and kill you without thinking about how lost I'll be without it. Understand?"

"I do, my lord." Frazier told her to call him Frazier. "I can do that too, sir. Yes. And I do make a good apple pie. The child and I are going to make you both up a dinner tonight that is sort of quick, but we'll do better from now on. You just leave us a list of things you won't eat, and we'll make sure to try things we don't have here too."

"I'm a shifter bear. As is my entire family. We will eat just about anything." Frazier looked at her and winked. "Well, my dear wife, we have staff now. That's even better than my other married brothers have. I have to go rub it in their faces."

With a kiss, he was gone. After talking to Tabby and Patty, she let them get to work. Since the meeting had taken so very little time, they had gotten back home well before dark. Going into the office that she'd claimed as her own, she set to work on finding the list of names that she was to mark through as being killed.

Before dinner was ready, the other two women came to work for them. Their names were Mary and Libby. She liked them both, and with such a huge house, Amelia thought they'd need the extra hands to keep up with it. Not that she couldn't use magic to clean it, but this would be so much better, she thought. There wouldn't be any cause for people thinking that she was using her magic for her own gain too. That was the biggest rule not to break, she'd always thought.

By the time she and Frazier were ready for bed, the dinner being better than she could have hoped for, she felt like she'd been doing her job forever instead of just tonight. Tomorrow she had another list of things to take care of. Also, she was going to go on a fall walk with grannie and the other two women to gather things for tea. Amelia was going to be hunting the earth for herbs that she could use for her magic.

Frazier was going to back to work tomorrow. She had a feeling that, like Mark, he'd be putting in his notice before too long. The park service was going to lose all the Cross men before too much longer if she didn't miss her bet. Once they had mates, they'd be working more from home and getting more in the way. Laughing to herself, she wondered how the newest bride for the men would be, hopefully, like the rest of them.

Just as she was dozing off, she felt her mother's presence. Not moving so as not to disturb Frazier, she asked her mom if she was coming back now that she'd done all the hard work.

"Listen to you being a smart ass. No, I'm not coming back. I've no reason to. The earth is happy with you too. You did a good thing in killing off the coven tonight. And making the earth heal faster was also the best way to go." She told her that it was Frazier's idea. *"Yes, he is much like you. A lover of all things earth. I see him working more and more with you in the coming years. He's a good person to have on*

your side if you were to ask me."

"He is. And you should see him pouring over the books that I've given him. I can see him helping me will all the bylaws when they are breached." She thought of something. *"Mom, do you suppose this is what it's like to have a mate with you when you're magical? That they not just enhance you when you need it but are able to pull you back when that's needed too? Tonight he did that for me. I was ready and willing to destroy the town that these women came from if not for him. Was that what father was to do for you?"*

"I believe so. But since I don't know, I can only assume, as you have, that is the way it should work." Mom sounded sad at that moment, and Amelia told her that she was sorry. *"Don't be child. I'm so happy for the two of you that I can hardly contain myself. If he's not working with you daily before the end of the fall season, I'll be surprised. But do allow him time to work too. His art, it's what saves him at times. He is also very good at it."*

"I will. He's going to be bringing some of his work into his home now. As are the others, I think. They're all so very talented, don't you think?" Mom said that they were. *"Good. I need some sleep, mother dearest. I love you and miss you more all the time. I'm so happy that you came to me tonight. Thank you for that."*

"'*Tis my pleasure, my child. My pleasure indeed.*" Once her mom was gone, she snuggled into Frazier's warmth and closed her eyes. Tomorrow was going to be good, she thought. Just what she'd needed and didn't know about. A good man at her side and a home and hearth to be happy in.

Chapter 5

Frazier put the miniature log cabin down and picked up the barn. He'd started off his morning with the barn and was frustrated with it, so he'd gone to the house. Looking it over, he saw what he was going wrong. Not only had two of the lightning poles fallen off someplace, but the door wasn't like the one that was on the barn here. He'd somehow put the wood going in the wrong direction.

He'd been working on the table for the store for about a year now. He was not working all that hard really but picking up a piece to put in it here and there when he was out working. Being quite proud of it so far today, he decided that it was time to get it finished or do something else entirely with the wood that he'd placed in the frame.

Grannie had asked him, well, all of them, for a large showpiece to put into the shop. So far, no one had done it, and he was feeling bad about it. When she'd asked him what his plans were for the day, then told him a nice table would be good, he decided to get on it as soon as he entered the shop. And so far, things had been going nicely for him. After fixing the wood planks he'd made himself, he put the barn down to dry and looked over at the pinecones he still had to form.

All he'd done to make them in miniature was to take one of the many scales that keep the seeds safe from weather and animals and shape it the way he wanted with his knives. He knew that having a lot of them, several hundred as a matter of fact, was going to take time, but he was going to make this setting look like it had been pulled right off the mountain. So far, Frazier thought he'd done about six hundred of them and decided that he was going to take a few scales in the house and work on them while watching television.

Frazier had seen something like the table he was working on online. The person had taken wood that had been thoroughly dried out and cut in to fit in the frame. His frame was fairly large for a table, but he'd been thinking at the time no one would want to buy it if it was this large. Then it would be at the store for a long time.

The wood was in two opposite corners of the frame. Taking up the upper and lower half of the mold so that when he was ready, he could fill in the empty space with his mountain scene. So far, in addition to the house and the barn, he had fashioned a garden with vegetables in it, such as corn and tomatoes. Also, he'd been able to figure out a way to make several bears, both brown and black, to be put in different places throughout the scene. The roadway was just a lot of sandstones, tiny rocks that he'd picked up pocketfuls as he'd been out on tours.

Pine, as well as other trees, had been made before, and he thought that he might have to add a few more to his collection before he was ready to start pouring resin in the mold. He was pleased too that he'd been able to make people too that were on the homestead that looked a great deal like his grandparents. There was even a little cemetery up near the hill where he'd put his parents' names on the markers.

When the door opened behind him, he knew it was his brother Mark. Telling him to come to have a look at what he was doing, Mark pointed out some of the things that Frazier had put down last year that he'd forgotten about.

"This is going to be magnificent. This is for the shop, isn't it?" Frazier told him that grannie had mentioned it this morning as he was leaving after talking to her. "I love the way that you've incorporated things from around the park in here too. Are you going to put a sign that says it's from the Smokies?"

"I thought about it but decided I'd just put a label on the end where it's not so noticeable. For some reason, I have it in my head that it would be somewhat distracting." Mark said he could see that. "Dexter is going to give me the little slivers of glass he has left over when he blows something I can use for windows if I want. Also, I thought they'd make great reflectors in the water too."

"I have to get going on my project too. Grannie wants me to make a couple of 3D maps of different parts of the park so she can put them out. I thought last year when she asked for them, I'd have no trouble with it. But now that I've sat down to think about it, it's not the work that will be hard. It's picking only a couple of places to do." Frazier asked him why he didn't just do them all. Add to it when he gets it done. "Don't you think that would take up a lot of space?"

All he had to do was point to the table mold, and Mark laughed. "This is going to be eight and a half feet by six feet when it's done. It'll more than likely weigh about a ton with the legs on it too. This is going to sit in the store forever because no one is going to put this sucker in a shopping bag and walk around town with it." They were both laughing when Gibb joined them.

"I can see that since you're working out here that Grannie hit on you about her project too. She wants me to get some starters from our property to put into pots to sell. Then she said when it's done for the season, if there are any left, she'll plant them around the shop, which will be nice too. I wonder if she thinks that people will actually buy herbs from the mountainside to take home."

Both he and Mark said yes at the same time. "It's a bit of fun for someone to have a plant that they got from around here. Besides, this way, they can legally take home some of the park and not be arrested when they're found out. Grandda is finding some small trees that he'll put in small pots for tourists. I'm not entirely sure how that will work. Trees aren't something that you can just put on a window sill if your weather doesn't support them. But grannie gets what she wants."

He was still working on some of the pine cones after showing Mark how to do them when grannie joined them. She had made some tea and was wondering if they'd try it for her. All of them simply loved her homemade teas and were more than glad to have a try. Today she and the women were going hunting for the flowers and other items that she needed to make more for the store.

Frazier had always loved the cornflower tea that she made. The pretty blue color of the water when it was seeping made him think of the blue skies in the summer months. It was why he'd had his brother Dexter, who blew glass for the shop, make him a set of clear glass tea cups so that he could enjoy the tea and the stunning colors.

"I have some cookies too that I'm going to be making as well. You all will try them after dinner, won't you?" Agreeing that they'd try anything that came out of her kitchen, she blushed a little. "You boys. I just don't know what I would have done without you here all these years. I'm so glad that we'll be taking our last breaths here, too, you know."

No one said anything, but Mark did get up to hug Grannie. Then it was a free-for-all with them all taking turns hugging her. She'd been down of late, and he and grandda had been talking about how she needed to be getting out more. A decision came to him then.

"I have an idea. Instead of you making dinner for all of us, why don't we order a bunch of Chinese food and bring it back here to have a feast? I know that grandda would leap at the chance to have some egg rolls and crab Rangoon for dinner. What do you think?" Mark suggested that so as not to overwhelm one restaurant, we make a list and divide it into the three places we loved so there would be plenty of food for us all to be stuffed. "I like that idea better. Yes, that's wonderful."

As they began listing off the things that they should order, grannie was making a list. It was quite extensive when they were finished, and most of the food was in the way of appetizers and such. They were going to see if they could get a gallon of hot sour soup from each place to eat. It was by far his favorite soup when he had a chance to get it. By the time grannie had the list worked up, she handed each one of them what they were to order. His comprised of being fifty egg rolls. He only hoped that a place could handle that many. He asked Mark about it.

"It's only nine in the morning. That should give them plenty of time, don't you think to get them made up or whatever they do to make them. Even if we don't get all we want, it would be plenty enough for us all to get at least one or two." Frazier looked at his brother. "All right, we should all get about four, but I was hoping for leftovers."

In the end, they were able to get the egg rolls and soup, but they weren't going to be able to get any dumplings. That disappointed all of them. It was perhaps his second most favorite thing when it came to eating Chinese food.

Frazier was glad about his progress when he was ready to leave to pick up his part of the food. Not only had he gotten the other three log cabins made and drying, but he'd been able to get all the pinecones that he thought he'd need to finish the table. Also, he'd been able to put in the first layer of resin, the support layer he called it, where he sat the things that were going to be in the 'water' to make sure that they stayed when the rest was poured in the mold.

While he was driving into town, he thought about the piece again. Where the water met the falls, he had several bears catching salmon to eat. So far, he'd been able to get the first layer of the fish painted in, and he was more than pleased with how that had turned out. Pulling into the lot where he was going, he heard from Amelia.

"I've had the best time today. And I'm to understand that we're having a feast of food too." He told her about where he was, and grannie had filled her in on the rest. *"I love your grannie so much, Frazier. She's so funny and honest. Oh, before I forget, the place where the car was is completely empty of the crime scene now. You'd never know that anything happened there unless you saw it. I'm glad that they did such a good job cleaning it up. I'd hate to have to turn someone into something because they left us a mess*

to clean up."

"I think that's what they were thinking. Only it was grannie that got on their asses. She told the local police that it wasn't of her making, and if they wanted us to find other things like this, then they'd better not make her regret it the first time." He could feel Amelia's laughter. *"I think that everyone in town is a little afraid of grannie. She doesn't take shit from anyone and won't put up with littering."*

He was a little early for the food, so he sat at the table reserved for to-go orders. Frazier asked Amelia if they were able to get enough flowers and such for grannie. She said that it helped them a great deal that she was able to find them with the help of the earth.

"We managed to get some things that she'd not been able to find for a while too. I had no idea that she hunts truffles, too, when she can. She said that her stupid pig got himself killed by a cougar one day, and she'd not been able to find them since. I tell you, the things that come out of her mouth in that sweet southern drawl are amazing." He smiled when his name was called. "I guess you're kind of busy picking up food. I'm nearly to town to make a trip to the store, too, so that I can get something to drink. Grannie told me to get gallons of sweet tea and unsweet tea so that we could all have something to drink." He told her that the only one that drank the sweet stuff was grannie and grandda and to not get more than two gallons of that. "I will. Thanks."

He and Mark got to the house at the same time. Amelia pulled in a few minutes later, and the two of them went out to help her bring in the tea. He was glad to see that she'd gotten ten gallons of unsweet because he was going to be able to take a couple home with them. Gibb showed up a few minutes after the table was laden with food with still several more bags to empty. He also had some great news.

"I got dumplings. I think maybe we all did, as a matter of fact. When I went to pick the stuff up, they told me that they'd gotten in a shipment today. Calling the other two restaurants, which I guess he owns, he told them to make sure they added some to our order since we were such good customers." Mark just pulled the tray of them out of the last bag when Gibb mentioned that. "I hope you have some too, Frazier. It's all I've been able to think about since I found out that we were getting them."

Not only did he have some as well, but they discovered that they had been given bottles of soy sauce as well as the sriracha sauce that his brothers loved as well. There was so much food on the table that they had to have trays to use their plates. But it was by far the best food he'd eaten in a while simply because of the company of his family with him. Frazier wondered what it would be like when the rest of the mates came and then the children. They'd have to eat outside with tables put together in a long row, he thought. And he'd enjoy that too.

~*~

"Do I know you?" Amelia had been followed by the woman that had finally spoken to her for the last hour. Every time she turned around, there she was. After finally asking her what the hell she wanted, she asked her if she knew her. Like that was not suspicious or anything. "I think I know you. Didn't we go to school together?"

"Doubtful. You're human." She started to turn away, and the woman grabbed her arm. "Don't touch me. Remove your hand from my person, or I will remove it from your wrist. You've no reason to touch me."

"You're not very nice, are you?" Amelia agreed with her, which through the woman off for a few seconds. Just enough time for her to step away from her. "I'm thinking that the only way to get what I want is to be straight up. I want you to call your friend here. I want to talk to Jamie Cross."

"No." Turning away again, she felt the gun or what she thought was a gun, jab her in the back. "You're really starting to piss me off here. Do you want to die? I've no trouble with that. I can even make it look like you killed yourself so I'd not end up in jail. I'm not going to call Jamie or anyone else here."

She did, however, reach out to Jamie. *"She's pretty insistent on having you come here. I'm not worried about her being able to kill me, but it will piss me off if I have to ruin my blouse. I like this one."* Jamie asked her where she was. *"Good point. You know that restaurant that has the giant skillet out in front? I'm about a foot from it. There was a commotion with some witchcraft that I came to — like you care. I'm there. Can you do that popping thing without being seen by her?"*

"*I can. I can see you both now. It's not a gun. It's a*

hairbrush. Also, you'll be thrilled to know that I haven't any idea who she might be. Let me do a little walk through her empty head." After a few minutes, she could feel Jamie's laughter. *"She wants me to use my dogs to help her find her cheating husband. She's a loon, Amelia. They've been divorced for nearly three years, and he came here to start a new life without her. I've seen this before, recently, as a matter of fact. If I can't have you sort of mentality, then no one will. I'm coming toward you from behind. Just don't kill her. She is seriously in denial about the divorce and the way that it ended. I'm nearly there."*

Turning around, Amelia grabbed the hairbrush at the same time. When the woman fell back on her ass, she put her foot on her chest and held her there. Jamie was calling the police as she was walking up on the two of them.

"I need for my husband to come and pick me up. He's not being fair to me. Did you know that he took my kids from me?" Jamie asked her if she'd really tried to kill them. "They were just a way to keep him with me, and he saved them. Isn't that the most precious thing in the world? He's such a good man but a little lost now. He needs me as much as I need him."

"You need help is what you need." The woman told them that she only needed her husband and was still going on about how she needed him when the police showed up. She begged them to go away so that she and Jamie had a contract for her to find her husband.

Frazier contacted her just as the woman, Porsche Miller, was being loaded up in the cruiser and taken away. After she told him what she'd been up to, he laughed, telling her that at least it ended well.

"I've got some great news. Well, I hope you think it's great news. I've decided to turn in my notice at work. I've never felt so relaxed as I have in the past week working on things that I want to do. Grannie is thrilled. She said that she'd hire me to work the shop a couple of days a week so that I can talk to the people about the park too." She told him that she was so happy for him. *"Me too. Talking to you last night about it really helped me solidify my answer for the job. It didn't help either that I've had a really rough day today with tourists."*

"I guess there is a lot of that going around. Harlin, you know, Jamie's dad had a tourist toss hot coffee at him today. Luckily he wasn't hurt too much, but it's still a shitty

way to have people treat you." He agreed with her. *"I'm headed to a meeting. I'm supposed to be meeting with the coven around here that is having issues. She wasn't too specific as to what her troubles were, but I guess I'll find out. Where are you?"*

"I'm at the ranger's office with Gibb. He has the desk today. I'm waiting on my next group to show up, then I'm going to —" When he stopped talking, she stopped walking. Jamie was with her, and she stiffened too. *"Can you and Jamie meet me at the north entrance of the park? There is a ranger down, and shots were fired."*

"I'll get you and take you with me." He said that he needed to drive in. *"No. I'll come and get you. You'll be safer than being on the road not knowing…do you know who it is?"*

"It's grandda." Popping into the bathroom at the office, she took him there first, then Gibb, who was closing up the office when she returned for him. They both were so upset that she told them she'd go and get grannie.

"I'm going to be just fine. He'll be all right when I get there, then I'm going to kick his bottom for making us all fuss after him." She could tell that the woman was upset but being brave. She'd heard that Grandda had been shot twice, but no one could get to him. "You tell him for me when we get there that I'm not going to wait around for him to die on me. Oh, Amelia, whatever will I do without him?"

"You'll be fine. Both of you will. I'll…I'm going to do something you asked me not to do for the two of you." Grannie only nodded and told her to do it. "All right. I can take it back if you decide you don't want to be here forever, but he'll live."

She didn't tell her that if he was already gone, there was nothing she could do for him. When she reached out, touching his mind with her own, it broke her badly to know it was too late. Grandda had died.

Grannie knew as soon as she did that he'd passed. They were mates, after all, and she knew the moment that he took his last breath. Holding onto Frazier as he realized the news, too, he sobbed so hard on her shoulder that she was at a loss as to how she could help him.

"Can't you go and get him, honey? He's just lying there, and I need to hold him one more time." She said that she could but was worried that the police would get pissy about moving him. "Yes, I guess they have to have their evidence on this. My poor Alford. Why did they shoot an old man like him?"

The man who had killed Grandda was killed by the rangers there. He'd killed three people, including Alford Cross, when he'd come to the park this morning. Now there was a man, a wonderful person, dead because the man couldn't get his credit card to work so that he could buy dinner for his family. He'd been drinking heavily since he'd arrived, and it didn't bode well for anyone, it seemed.

After the man was killed, not soon enough for the family, Grandda was taken to the hospital and pronounced dead before they arrived. Grannie had been able to sit with him for as long as she wanted, and the family gathered around her.

When she consented to have him taken to the mortuary, she didn't move from her seat in the emergency department. None of them wanted to rush her either. Amelia thought that it would be a very long time before any one of them was ready to face the world without one of the greatest men she knew.

"I'd like to go home now." Mark took her home

as he was the only one with a car there. Grannie leaned heavily on her grandsons, and it hurt her heart in ways that she couldn't explain. "When we get there, I want you all to please stay with me for a bit. I'm...my mind is a bit scrambled right now, but I'd very much like to have you all there."

No one said that they had things to do. Not that she thought they would, but it showed how much love and respect they had for her when they all told her that they'd be there for as long as she could stand them. The ride back to the homestead was quiet. Grannie cried softly in her lacy handkerchief and talked about some of the things that the two of them had done while first married. Once they were home, she sat in her usual chair and looked at Amelia.

"I don't want you to give me that immortality, child." The family was mourning the death of their patriarch badly. Grannie was taking it the hardest, of course, and it was all she could do not to beg her not to die. "I want to go with him. To the great mountains in the sky. He's my heart, and now that he's gone, I don't think it will ever beat the same."

No one begged her not to leave them. It was as if

they knew, deep in their hearts, that it wouldn't matter what they said to her. Her mind was made up. And Amelia knew too that she'd never be the same now. As she had said, her heart was broken.

"Mine and your Grandda's will is all made up. I'll tell you now that it will be equally divided between the six of you. There's a bit of money along with some jewels that had been passed down to us over the years that I'd like to have you give to the women in the family as they come along." Mark told her that he'd do that for her. "Thank you, son. Also, I want you to know that you've never been a burden on us. We'd do it all over again, even knowing what we know now. You've been the best grandsons that a person could ask for, and I don't want you to ever think any differently."

"Words aren't enough to tell you how much we love you, grannie." She took Frazier's hand into hers and kissed the back of it. "We'll tell our children about you too. They'll think they knew you by the time they're ready to have their own children."

"Now, don't you be making me out to be some kind of saint, young man. You know as well as I do that I have me a powerful temper and I let it go on occasion."

They all laughed, and grannie smiled at them. "That's just what I needed. To hear a little laughter right about now."

"What do you want us to do about grandda's funeral? I know that you had your arrangements made, so you tell me if you want anything different." Grannie told Gibb that it was the way they wanted it. "We'll abide by your wishes then."

"Yes, please do that." She looked around the big room, the home that Mark had been living in since he'd met Jamie. Smiling at them, tears streaming down her face, she told them how much she loved them and then stood up. So did everyone in the room with her. "I'm powerful tired right now. I think I'll go and have me a nice nap. Then we'll talk some more."

Amelia and the other two women helped her change her clothing. It was smeared in blood when she'd been able to hold onto Grandda while the police finished up their day. As they were leaving the room, she looked back at the woman and thought that she'd never looked her age until just that moment. It was Sunny that spoke first.

"She'll be gone in the morning. You know that,

don't you guys? She's broken in ways that I can only imagine. I love that old buzzard so much. I know you two do as well." They all nodded, holding onto each other as they sobbed about how they'd miss her. "She's been such a wonderful person to all of us. I just don't think things will ever be the same without the two of them right there all the time."

Entering the living room with the men, she sat on the couch with Frazier and the others. Quietly, one by one, they left, leaving only Mark and Jamie there to watch over grannie when she took her last breath. There was no doubt in any of their minds that she'd not be here long without her mate Alford.

Chapter 6

The entire town turned out for the funerals. Frazier hadn't realized until today how far-reaching his grandparents had been to the community and beyond. There were other rangers from other parks there that told him how either his grandmother or grandfather had helped them in some way that put them where they were today. One particular story still had him smiling a little, even hours later. David Clancy had been the storyteller then.

"You and your brothers had gone off to go fishing with your granddaddy. I was a mean little shit back then. Tormenting people and animals until I ever got caught or bored. I was at your house, and I had already seen where the six of you were gone, so I found me a stick and was tormenting that old raccoon that lived up under your porch. You remember her, Fraz, don't you?" He told David that her name had been Bonny. "That's right. Bonny. Well, she was getting pissy with me on account of me poking at her with my stick when your grandmammy came out there. All she did was put out her hand. I knew better than to mess with her. So I handed over the stick. She went and broke it over her knee. But she hesitated just enough where I was fearful that she was going to use that stick on me like I had been Bonny."

David had been a terrible child right up until one summer. After that, he was about the best kid around to have in your corner. He was kind to animals too. Taking his little sister to school and making sure that she had her lunch money. David's father was a drunk, and a mean one at that and he never did anything for his family but died young and left them alone. Frazier thought he heard that the man had fallen off his porch, drunker than anything and had frozen to death. No one put up much of a fuss about it, and the Clancy family never had the police pulling up in their yard again.

"Your Grandmammy, she asked me if I'd ever

seen a baby possum before. I told her no. Then I asked her if they were as ugly as their mammy? Boy, don't you know that she smacked me hard enough to knock me to my ass? I stayed right there too. Then she tells me that all babies are beautiful if you take the time to get to know them." David shook his head as he continued his story. "Won't you know it, Fraz, she called Bonny out from under that porch and had her sit right on her lap. Then she told me…well, she told me how I was a good boy that just nobody cared enough to tell me that."

David looked away, and Frazier wiped at his own tears. He knew what had happened after that. His grannie would spend the next two years tutoring David on his reading and math. He would just show up about supper time, eat supper with them, work on his studies and then go home. His clothing would be clean along with anything that he might have brought over for his little sister Kimmy too. After a few months of David joining them, Kimmy started showing up as well, bringing more laundry and going home with a sack of food to feed their mother. David hugged him before he finished his story.

"I'm a good vet because of her taking the time to show me that all babies are beautiful. Your grandmammy had a heart of gold, I tell you, Frazier. Kimmy is a doctor too. Got her a good husband and nice family living in a good clean house. I wish every day, every single day, that I'd been able to show your grandmammy how much she meant to me." Frazier said that he had. "How do you figure? I got me a good education and never looked back."

"Do you do a good job, David? When you're working with your clients, do you treat them right? Do your wife and children know how much you love them? Every day? Do you pay it forward? What my grannie did for you, do you help someone else in the same way?" He said he did. Several times a day, even if it's to only help someone get their pets healthy. "Then you thanked her. That's all she would have wanted, David. For you and your sister to make sure that you helped anyone and everyone that needed it just like she did for you and Kimmy. Who I heard just last week performed heart surgery on a child for free because they didn't have the money to get it done otherwise. That is my grannie's legacy, David. The one that you just told me about. Thank you for that. You've made my heart lighter with your story."

Frazier thought of that first night. The night that his grandda had been killed. And his Grannie had gone off to bed. He'd been lying in bed beside Amelia when he felt his grannie's passing. It was just after midnight, and his heart shattered in his chest just as she took her last breath. Getting up, he knew that Amelia was awake, so all he said to her was that he had to go find his brothers. She told him that she loved him and he told her that he loved her too.

Mark was the first brother that he saw. He'd been sitting on the porch swing moving back and forth, crying softly. When the others showed up, they, too, sat on the porch with them. Frazier wanted to go into the house. To see if it were true that she'd died with grandda. But he didn't. This way, he told himself, without looking, he could pretend for one more minute that she was still with them. Mark cleared his throat before speaking to them in a hushed tone.

"I've not called anyone yet. I...I don't know why, but I just couldn't." They heard a rustling in the yard beyond what they could see with the porch light on. Mark stood up first and cautioned them. "Don't anyone move."

As the bears came into the light, dozens of them, it looked like none of them made a move toward the porch where they were. There were families of them as well as single bears that looked to be younger than a year old. The first bear, who seemed to be older than any of the others, bowed his head at them and wandered slowly off into the woods. For the next forty minutes or so, each bear that came into the light did the same thing, as if they too were hurt that the two people who had lived here as long as they had had passed onto the great bear mountain in the sky.

None of them spoke of what they'd just witnessed. He doubted that if they had told the story to anyone that there would be one person that would believe them. Hundreds of bears, black and brown, came that night and through the next morning to pay homage to their grandparents. Now here they were on the last day of calling hours for the same people that the bears had loved. People were here to do the same.

Others had similar stories like David's to tell. Most of the people he knew in passing. Others simply came by because they knew one of them. Tomorrow morning they were going to lay them to rest in a private ceremony on the land where other family was lain, including his parents.

They'd had to open up the high school to use it as a place to lay out his grandparents for the showing. There had been so many flowers and gifts taken to the funeral home that first day that it became necessary to find them a bigger venue. The only thing that they did differently to grannie and grandda's wishes was to have an extra few hours of calling hours. Grannie and grandda had thought that they'd outlived anyone that would care that they passed on. They both had been so very wrong.

After the ceremony on the hill, they met at Mark's home again. There were hundreds of plates of food. Tupperware filled with cakes and cookies. All of them with a small piece of tape on them with the last name of the person that had brought them.

Plastic glasses to use along with napkins and plasticware. So many crockpots plugged in he did worry for a bit if they were going to overload the house. The trays of vegetables were nice. Homemade dips were with them. He also noticed that there were buckets of chickens from the local chicken place. Gallons of tea, both sweet and unsweet. Mark said that he'd told people to come back here to have some food, and it seemed they brought some for everyone.

Walking around the room where all the planters had been put, he and Amelia read the cards that were with them. Again, he didn't know some of the names, but others, like the President of the United States, he was surprised the man had found out. All the cut flowers had been donated to the church where they'd gone to be redone and sent to nursing homes.

It was Dexter that came up behind him this time. They'd been hugging each other all morning, and it felt like a good way to tell each of them that they had their back. Dexter then asked him if he could talk to him about something. They made their way out to the back deck and sat down.

"I've given my notice to the park. So have Mark and the others. I don't—no, that's not it, I can't work there anymore. It's just too much." Frazier said he'd given his notice the morning that grandda had been killed. "Yes, Mark told me. I can't go to work there anymore when the tourist are armed better than we are. Not that they should be, but it's a different world out there than it had been when we started. Violence is the first thing that some people jump to when things don't go their way. I can't…every time I think of seeing my grandda there on the ground because some idiot's card wouldn't work, I just can't do it. It's just too much for my heart to take."

"I understand. I really do." They didn't say anything for several minutes, and it seemed all right for them both. "Dexter, what are your plans? I'm sure you've thought this through all the way to the end. We're going to be living for a great long time, and we can't just give up on things because they're harder now. I mean, that's what I was just thinking about."

"I might go back to the Park someday. But for now, I need to get my own heart working. I feel like I've had all the stuffing taken out of me. If not for Sunny, I'm not sure what I'd be doing today." He knew that feeling as well. "We're going to try and have a child. Right away. I don't know what Mark and you have planned, but I want to bring children into this world and bring them up on this mountain. Show them everything that we learned while children here at the feet of the two most wonderful people in the world."

"Dexter, what is really wrong?" He knew his brother well enough to know that he wasn't saying what was really wrong. Whatever it was, he was more than just a little upset about it, and Frazier could wait until he was ready before he told him to chill. "You're acting like the world is against you. I don't think it is."

Dexter got up and paced a bit. The air was turning chilly, but it didn't bother either of them. It was the fact that his brother was wearing shorts that told him his anger was making him hot. As Dexter stretched his neck twice and popped his shoulders, he finally sat down in the chair again and looked reasonably calmer than he had before.

"I don't want to live here anymore. I want to get off this mountain and live in a city." Frazier didn't know what to say, so he said nothing. "I hate it here now. I mean, I don't even want to go into town to be around anyone anymore. Frazier, I've never felt like this before in my life, but I want to grab my gun, go into town and start shooting people who are arguing about stupid shit. That's not like me."

"No, it's not." Not sure where this was coming from. The violence was so palpable right now from his brother he asked him what Sunny had said. "You've spoken to her, right? I'm not saying that she'd change your mind or anything, but you've told her how you feel, haven't you?"

"No. I mean, she knows that I'm pissed off, but I've not…she'll be pissed off at me and tell me that once I'm calmer, it'll go away. The need to run around like a lunatic, I mean." He asked him if he wanted the feelings to go away. "Damn it, Frazier, I want you to yell at me and tell me that I'm stupid or something. I don't want you to try and see what's in my head."

"Now you're being an idiot." Dexter got up and started pacing again. "You wanted me to talk you out of leaving, didn't you? So if it didn't work out, you'd be able to blame me for this."

"No." He stood there for several minutes before speaking again. "Yes. I guess I did. I really don't want to leave, but I also don't know if I'll be able to take living here without Grandda and Grannie."

"Can I ask you something without you going off the handle?" He told him he didn't know anymore.

"Fair enough. What do you think they'd say if they heard you right now? I mean, besides grannie hitting you upside the head for being so dramatic, what do you think they'd say?"

"Honestly?" Frazier told him, of course. "They'd tell me to get my head out of my ass and think about the fact that they were both older than dirt and that they were going to die anyway. But Grandda was killed."

"Yes. He was. Doing something that he loved doing." Dexter turned to him. "Did you read the report? The one that the police have? It says that Grandda was protecting two children who were in the line of fire when the man went off. They'd be dead right now if not for him shielding them. He died, just as I said, doing something that he loved doing. Not just protecting the park but the people that came here to have a good time. To see a bear. Buy things that they have no need for. Grandda went to work every day, knowing that it could be his last. Grannie too. They were in their nineties, Dexter. And they loved one another more than they did anything in this world." He snorted before continuing. "I think it's the most loving and the most romantic thing a couple could do is to know, deep in their hearts, that they couldn't live without one another."

"You're a sap." He grinned at him. "I guess you're right. And I think I knew that when I came to you that you'd be talking to me instead of talking me out of anything. Mark would have slapped me around. Barron would have ignored me and told me that I was stupid. The others? Yeah, they'd do the same. But I knew that you'd just make me see the sense of it all."

"You're welcome." Hugging his brother, he held on a little tighter than he would normally have done. When they released each other, he looked at his brother and saw that he was indeed feeling better. "I think it's great that you and Sunny are going to have a kid or two. Maybe by the time the other mates come along, we'll all have some cubs around too."

"I'd like that. Very much." Getting another hug from his brother, they both sat down and talked about their grandparents. He was going to miss them both, they all were, but he knew too that they were together and that to him mattered more than him having a broken heart because they were gone.

~*~

Amelia had a whole new respect for her mother. She also understood why she stopped having these monthly meetings with the witches in charge of a coven in part of the United States. The ones in charge were nothing but a whiny bunch of bitches that no more deserved her time than she wanted to give it to them. When someone nudged at her from a link, she paused in her nearly destroying the witch in front of her. Pausing, she thought it was a good thing too. Otherwise, she might well have enjoyed herself too much and taken out the entire room.

"You're in a mood today." She smiled when it was Jamie that spoke to her. *"My goodness, what is she going on about? Something about housing. I wouldn't think you guys would have that much trouble with housing. Just poof, you have a house."*

"We can't use our magic to make our lives easier. Not that everyone doesn't do this already to a small degree, but there is a limit even on what I will approve. This one, in particular, is wholly aware of what the rule is but has been working on loopholes — that I must admit are pretty clever — to get her neighbor to turn over her house to her. It's bigger, she says and just what she needs to hold her monthly

meetings. But it's the appliances, as well as the large master bedroom, that she wants more. Also, there is a grand pool out back that she thinks her family will enjoy more than hers would. It's not going to happen. What can I do for you, my dear friend?"

"You know what I did for the government, right?" She asked her if she was still working for them. "When they beg and pay me a shit ton of money, I'll work for them. In this one, Sunny is going to help me out as well. She has this freaky ability that allows her to change into the littlest things and get in and out. Anyway, I digress. I need your help with the earth. I could have asked Frazier because he can do it too, but he's having entirely too much fun, and you're not."

"No, I'm not. However, I do feel as if I'm missing something here. Like I'm being tested or something." Jamie asked her to hold on. She'll look. After a few minutes of asking Mable questions, Jamie spoke to her again. "You're kidding? I know you're not, but I can see my mother doing this. Every day I find things that I'd like to take her to task about. I wouldn't, but there are days. So they want to piss me off with bogus requests so that I will get so fed up and tell them I didn't care what they did. Slick workaround *if you can get them to make me pissy. Which I am, but now I'm going to be here all fucking day and dowl out charges against them until this is finished. In the meantime, I can help you too. Whatever you need."*

"Great. There is a visitor in town who is making issues. Usually, I wouldn't care, but when I had to go into town earlier this morning, he nearly knocked me down when he stomped by me. I got like a reading from him. He's looking for his sister and her kid. I haven't any idea why he's pissy about that. His mind was too focused on finding them rather than why." She asked Jamie if she had a visual of him. *"I do. Frazier said you work better when you have something like that. When he turned around to cuss me out, I got a good look at his face and the gun he was packing. He's not anymore, by the way. I had Sunny take it from him. She couldn't get a read on him either. He is seriously pissed off right now."*

"Okay. You think of him, and I'll have a look. From there, I can trace him backward to — how far do you need me to go?" Jamie told her that at least until she found out what his anger was about. *"If I see the face of his sister or her kid, I'll go that route as well. Can you…I don't know. Keep listening to this woman and hint at what I should be saying when she pauses?"*

"Does she ever pause?" They both laughed, and she said that she'd do it. *"Thanks for this. I hope you can at least find out something."*

She found the man sitting in a restaurant having a cup of coffee. Amelia hated coffee with a passion. While she was drinking hot tea with Frazier nightly, she didn't care all that much for it either. Unless it was his grannies. She'd not asked for any of it, thinking they'd want to keep it around, but she could go for some of her fall special right now.

Getting into his mind, she found that he was an angry sort of shit. While searching for the cause of his over-the-top anger, she looked around for his reason for wanting to find his sister. It could be nothing more than she was a bitch and had said something to him this morning, but she—just as she was making up stories that might have pissed the man off, she found the source of his anger.

"Jamie?" She said she was there. *"There is a body in a gully near the entrance to the Pigeon Forge area. Not far from the mile marker that leads people back to Gatlinburg. He's been there for a while, at least a couple of months.*

Decomposed and been shot three times. There won't be any identification on him, but his name is Nathan Webb. He's the ex-husband of Dave Farley's sister. He's the angry shit. I can't find where he killed his brother-in-law, but he does know where his body is."

"That has him angry? Oh well, that's the man that I was supposed to find anyway. Webb has been missing from his home for about that long too." Amelia said she was still looking. *"You might want to tune into your meeting first. Mabel is thinking that you're agreeing with her proposal for her to take the house. Lay down the law if I were you and tell her how it's not going to happen."* Amelia looked at Mabel.

"I think you've gone on about this quite enough, Mabel. You will live in the house that belongs to you and leave your neighbor alone. If I hear that you are tormenting her again, I will have you pay a hefty fine for pestering her about anything at all." She looked around the room. "If you think that I'm going to do what my mother has done in the past, then you are sadly mistaken. I will hear each and every case, and I will, good or bad, pass judgement on you. If you are here to waste my time, to piss me off so that I walk away? You don't know me very well. I will be here until every appearance is heard. Do I make myself clear?"

Six of the witches gathered up their things and left. Two more were nodding like they were happy this was the way she was going to handle things from now on but left as well. As the eight remaining witches sat there, Amelia told them that she wasn't going to be listening to anyone wanting to increase their wealth by means of magic. That was against their bylaws. In the end, everyone in the room left, and she was finally able to concentrate on the man.

"Thanks for leading me right to Webb. Now if you could find out where Farley's sister is, and she's all right, I'd feel a good deal better. I have no idea why but I have a feeling that this isn't going to bode well for her in the end. Not if he's that angry still after a couple of months." Amelia told her that she'd found the source of his anger. *"I'm not going to like it, am I?"*

"Probably not. Nathan was an attorney for Madeline Farley, Dave's sister, in getting her child support for the kid. She goes by — hang on. She has three children, triplets. Two daughters and a son. Anyway, Maddy needs her child

support. Baby daddy is behind by about eight years now. Burney Archer just stopped working above board so that he'd not have to pay her for the kid's needs. Nathan and Maddy have been friends since before they started kindergarten together." She asked if she knew why her brother killed him. *"Dave has never liked Webb. He's smart and has been helping his sister hide from him. Why hiding? I don't see it in his mind, but I'm assuming that it has something to do with the fact that he knows Archer from prison. Really well, it seems."*

"So this shit killed the attorney that is helping his sister get food on the table for his two nieces and nephew because he didn't like him? You do know that is one of the stupidest reasons I've ever heard for a reason to kill someone, don't you?" Amelia laughed and said for as long as she's been around, that one is way up on the top of her list too. *"Do you happen to know where Maddy and the kids are? I mean, is he even in the right area to find them?"*

"Let me have a search around. She's a pretty little thing." Amelia found the woman easily enough, but finding the kids was a little more difficult. Each time the woman bounced from hiding place to hiding place, she didn't have the children with her. Being ten, she

figured that they'd have a good handle on being able to care for themselves, but she really didn't know that many children. *"She's good at hiding them away, that's for sure. And she is in town. She works three jobs right now, each of them a restaurant — to which there is an incredible amount of them around here. Dishwasher for two of them, and she cleans rooms for a bed and breakfast just up the road from where her brother is enjoying coffee."*

"I have him now. One of the officers that are helping me today is going to be watching him for the next few hours. By tonight he won't be able to take a shit without the Feds knowing the weight, size and what it consisted of. He's staying at one of the larger hotels just off the main drag in Gatlinburg." Amelia said she'd not known that she had that much pull. *"Neither did I, to be honest, but once I told them that he killed Webb, a federal judge, they stepped right in and took over. Fine by me."*

Still looking for the kids, she found four other hiding places they'd been hiding in over the last month. Each time they moved, it was as if they knew that Dave was close on their tail. Sometimes the kids would simply bug out of a hiding place before their uncle showed up an hour later. Never any less than that, either. Just as she was moving to the next place, she hit paydirt.

"*Found them. Christ, Jamie. They're behind the Gatlinburg Crockett's Breakfast Camp. It's on Parkway. They're going to be caught if — never mind. They heard some kid taking the trash out or something and have hidden again. They're all right, but I'd really like it if you were to pop there and get them. Take Mark with you. I don't want any of you hurt because they're digging in the dumpsters.*" She watched as the kids seemed to know just what they were looking for. "*They're smart as tacks, those three. Or their mother taught them well. Either way, they're not just eating people's leftovers from their plates. They've found some pancake mixes that are expired. Also, they've found a bag of apples, some other spices and some kind of canned meat. I think it's ham. Now they have some syrup that they're putting in their backpacks.*"

"*Do you know where they are headed?*" She told her that they'd been staying in one of the many empty shops along that lane. "*Okay. I'm going to go up Parkway and pop there ahead of them. This might turn out badly if they scream or something. What are you going to do?*"

"*Get their mom. I'll get her and then bring her with*

me to meet up with you guys. I just realized that one of the girls is hurt. I don't know how or anything. I'm focusing more on keeping up with Maddy for now." Jamie said that sounded like a good idea. *"I'll see you soon."*

Amelia used her considerable magic to close up the building she was in as she made her way to the restaurant where Maddy was working. Just as she was ready to come out of the bathroom where she had popped, a shot was fired in her direction.

She couldn't leave with Maddy. She'd been shot by someone coming from the dining area. It looked like she would bleed out if someone didn't get their heads out of their asses, so Amelia entered the brouhaha and started barking orders. No one seemed to understand that she didn't work there but did what she told them. Telling Jamie what was happening, she gave her just enough magic to keep her alive.

"Maddy has been shot twice. It's going to be touch and go here for a little bit. She was shot once in the head and then in the chest. Get the kids, and I'll meet you at the hospital." Jamie asked if she thought she'd be a while. *"Not on my end. But there is…Oh damn, Jamie. I found your man. He's dead. And it looks like Dave boy shot and*

killed him. His sister too. I'm so sorry."

"*Are you coming in the ambulance with her?*" She said that she could. "*I'll make sure that you can. Just be careful. He's on the run again, I'm assuming. We'll find him. And when we do, he's going to pay. I'm with the kids. I will have to tell them something so that —*"

"*Hang on. Maddy is talking to me.*" Leaning down to hear what she had to say, Amelia told her that they were picking up the kids right now. Nodding, she told her the word that she'd have to know in order for them to believe her. Once she had given it up, Maddy closed her eyes. Amelia gave the young woman a bit more magic to help her and spoke to Jamie. "*Tell them that their mother is hurt and going to live, but the code word for them to trust you is…you're not going to believe this, Jamie, but it's 'Minnie.' Just that. Minnie.*"

Chapter 7

Thad didn't have any idea why he trusted the people that had…well, his mind wouldn't allow him to think too hard about how they'd gotten to the hospital. The big man, his name was Mr. Gibb, had wrapped his arms around his waist, and they were suddenly at the hospital. He might well have hurt the man, even if he'd only been able to kick him, but his sisters were there too and didn't seem to be in any kind of fear. The two people holding onto them were Miss Sunny and Miss Jamie. He looked over at the man who had entered the emergency department by the sliding door. Like a normal person would, he wanted to point out but didn't.

"My name is Mark Cross. This is my wife, Jamie,

who has helped you. This is my sister-in-law Sunny and my brother, but not her husband, Gibb. You've introduced yourself to them?" All three of them told him that they had. "Good. All right. My sister-in-law Amelia is with your mom. They're on their way in by ambulance right now. Did you know that your mom had been hurt?"

"Yes, sir." Thad looked at his sisters when they nodded at him. He didn't know if this was a good idea or not, but they had all agreed. "We've been on the run for a bit now. Mom is about a step ahead of her brother all the time. We've been moving around a lot, so no one could find us. Dave, that's his name. He's not a very nice person. Is mom going to be all right?"

"Yes. She's in good hands. In the event that you didn't notice, we're all magical. Amelia is a witch and is staying next to your mom while she's there. She won't allow anything to happen to her while she's being taken care of. All right?" Thad nodded and looked at his sisters Belle and Maria again. "I've been told that one of you is hurt. This is a good time to be fixed up while we're here. No one will get to the four of you while we're with you. And we're not leaving you at all."

"Belle has been hurt. She hurt her ankle two nights ago when we were on the run. I tried to wrap it up for her, but it's still hurting her." Belle showed Mark her ankle when he asked. All he did was touch it, and Belle didn't seem to be in pain anymore. "Thank you for that. She's been hurting so much that I was worried about her. Does that work for all kinds of stuff, Mr. Mark?"

"Yes. Are you hurt?" He wanted to tell him that he was hungry, and that hurt too, but he knew that wasn't what he meant. So all he did was lift his pant leg up to show him the wound on his leg that was still bleeding through the paper towel. Thad had been keeping it clean with paper towels since the night it had happened. The infection was nasty smelling, and he'd get all sweaty at night when it hurt the worse. "That's a nasty cut, Thad. How did you get that? If you don't mind me asking."

"We were almost caught a couple of weeks ago. Mom was going to get me something to put on it today, she got paid, but I guess her brother caught up with her. I got hurt because I was going back to get the food that we'd left when we ran just when Dave showed up. He was really mad that he'd missed us again. I got cut from coming out of a screened-in window." He was never going to call Dave uncle again. The man had been tormenting them since he and his sisters were little. All on account of the little bit of something that the three of them had and he wanted them to work for him. It was Maria that started talking to Mark then.

"We can see things. Not really anything that is important to us. Contests, mom calls them, like ball games and horse races. We see who the winner is. We can also see the score or times the horses come in to win on the contest too. You know, when it's over." Mark didn't say anything as he pulled the paper towel completely off his wound. "But Belle, she can see when we're going to be caught, and we move then. It's only a little bit of time, but bugging out all the time is hard to do."

"I just bet it is." Jamie looked at his leg then. "That really is a nasty cut. However, I'd feel better if you were to get it cleaned up before we fix you up. All right? I mean, there might be something in the wound that will only keep festering. No one will know that you're here nor that you're hurt. I won't even tell your mom until she's better. If that's okay?"

"Yes. I don't want her to worry. She hates leaving us to get some work, but we need stuff too. Food is most important, I guess. We've gotten good at knowing who throws out the best things we can eat." Having someone helping them, even if they were strangers, nearly made him cry he was so relieved. He and his sisters had been trying so hard not to show their mom how afraid they were, and he thought that was stressing them out more. "Mom had to take us back from him about a year ago. It was our birthday, and he'd been in the house. I don't think he'd been invited or anything. He just came into the house and beat the snot out of our mom. After he drugged us, he took us to the racetrack and made us tell him the winners and stuff. It's cheating, and we know it, so we didn't want to help. Mom got us from him with the help of her friend Nathan. My biological father, he's a deadbeat and owes mom a lot of money that could be going for us having insurance and a car to get around in. I don't know why we'd need either of those, but mom sure does think it would make a difference for us."

Thad realized how angry he sounded and apologized to Mr. Mark. He told him he'd be angry too if someone that is supposed to be caring for him didn't do their job. Then he told him that they'd be staying with him and his wife until they could get to the bottom of things. He looked at his sisters to see if they were all right with that and noticed that Belle was staring at Mr. Gibb.

"What's wrong?" Thad didn't know what he could do to the man if he was going to hurt them, but they knew how to run, and they would too if it came to his sisters being safe. "Belle? What's wrong? Has he hurt you in any way?"

"No. Not at all." She finally looked at him. "We should stay with Mr. Gibb. He needs to get to know us all better."

Thad didn't know what was happening, but if Belle told him that he needed to boil his toes in oil, he'd do it. She'd never been wrong about stuff before. Maria could, too, tell them when they'd be safe someplace, but not nearly as often as Belle did.

"Gibb?" He only looked over at his brother and shrugged. It was then that Mr. Mark burst out laughing.

"I think I get it. All right. As soon as Maddy gets here, we'll test out this theory. All right?"

Mr. Gibb only smiled and looked at the three of them. Again he didn't know what was going on, but he figured that sooner or later, he'd talk to Belle and find out what was going on. When the big doors opened to the sound of sirens, he stood up with his sisters. His leg was hurting so bad by then that he nearly fell. And would have had Mr. Gibb not grabbed him up and held him in his arms. It was their mom.

"They're going to take her right up to surgery, and then they'll admit her." The woman that had been getting out of the ambulance came to kneel in front of them. "You must be, Thad. And your sisters are Belle and Maria. Your mom was so worried about you that she made me promise that I'd keep an eye on you all for her. I know that this is a great deal to put on you right now, but you couldn't be in better hands than you are with my family."

"I trust them too." A nurse came to get him and Mr. Gibb. "I have a cut on my leg that they're going to look at. I don't want my mom to know until she's better."

"Good idea." She looked up and over his shoulder at Mr. Gibb. "I think that all of you should be checked out while you're here. What do you think, Gibb? That way, when your mom is better, and she will be, we can tell her that you're all in the best of health."

"Excellent. What do you say, girls? Ready to make sure that you're all healthy with your brother?" His sisters followed him back to the emergency room. Once they were back there, it was as if there wasn't anyone else in the world around but the four of them to be seen. He was taken to x-ray after being put in a gown. "While you're gone, Thad, I'll see about getting a bigger room so that the three of you can be together while here."

Thad couldn't help it. He started to cry. It was so wonderful to have someone taking over all the things he'd been doing since he and his family had been on the run. Mr. Gibb didn't say anything while he held him but told Belle and Maria that stress and pain would make even grown men upset. After a few minutes of just holding onto someone stronger and willing to help them, he was taken to the other department to see about his leg.

When he got back to his room, there were two more beds in the room with his sisters on them. Belle was asleep, and Maria was looking at what he thought was Mr. Gibb's phone. He was in so much pain that she could have been looking at how to kill someone for all he cared.

"Hang on, Thad. They're going to bring you something for pain." He said that he couldn't leave his sisters. "I won't leave them. Nor you. You just let them give you something for the pain then you'll be able to rest. They're going to take you up to surgery in a few minutes to clean up that wound and make sure that the infection is taken care of. You're going to be just fine. I promise you."

He didn't want to question him about how he was going to make that happen. But he was worried. As soon as the nurse came in, she said that she was going to start an IV on him and he'd get something for the pain. Almost as soon as she told him he was going to feel a pinch, it was all over. Then she told him that he was going to feel drowsy but not to fight it. Thad thought that it was the most amazing thing in the world when she told him to close his eyes.

When he woke up, he was in a different room. There were three beds in the room, his sisters were in them sleeping and a big chair. He looked around the room, not entirely sure how he'd gotten in here, when he saw Mr. Gibb sitting in the chair next to his bed.

"I can talk to you like this if you want. Belle told me that you guys can talk to each other through a link as well." Thad asked him how he'd gotten in here. *"Your surgery went fine. You're on the mend. The doctor said you'd need to stay here for a couple of days before he was ready to release you because of the infection. But you're going to be just fine."*

Again the urge to cry rolled over him. Mr. Gibb sat up in the chair more and took his hand into his. He told him he was all right to be brave sometimes, but now he only needed to get well.

"Your mom is doing better too. They removed the bullets, and she's resting. In the morning, they're going to put her into a room where you guys can go and see her. She might not be awake fully, but she'll be here for a few more days longer than you will be." He asked where they were going to be staying. *"I have a big house on my family's land that you and your sisters will be able to go to. My family lives on a mountain that has been in our family for*

generations. I do want to talk to you about something. Do you know what a shifter is?"

"Yes." He looked at the big man. *"You're one, aren't you? All of your family — that's why Mr. Mark said you were all magical. You're a shifter too."*

"Yes, I'm a bear. A black bear. All of my brothers are. The reason that I'm asking you about this is that your mom is my mate. Do you know what that means?" He nodded, then shook his head. *"She and I are like husband and wife. But I want you to know that I won't ever harm her. Nor will I allow someone else to hurt her either. My entire family will protect you all with their lives."*

"Do you think that someone will — my uncle, Dave? He'll come after us again, won't he?" Mr. Gibb nodded. *Then told him what he thought. "He won't give up until he gets killed? You think he'll be like that?"*

"Money, especially free money coming to him with you guys helping, will make everyone greedy. Greedy men and women will go to great links, even killing someone related to them to get what they think they need or deserve." Thad asked him how far he'd go. *"I wouldn't have to. I have a great deal of money, Thad. And in saying that, you and your family do as well. If Dave won every horse race from now*

until he's dead, he'd not have nearly as much money as I do. I'm a very wealthy man. As are all my brothers and their families."

"Mom said we don't have two pennies to rub together." He smiled at him and told him she wouldn't have to worry about that anymore. *"You don't know my mom. She worries about everything. Even before we started running, we had some money. But she'd worry about a rainy day coming around. Sheesh, women are strange, don't you think?"*

"I'm not going to answer that. If your mom were to hear us talking about her like this, she'd brain us both, I think." Thad laughed. It felt good. Also, like a weight as big as him had been taken off him. *"All right, buddy. You need to get some rest. We're all going to be staying here until you can go home with us. My sisters-in-law are taking care that your rooms are set up nicely and that you have clothing to wear for the next few days. After that, we'll be playing it by ear until your mom is awake."*

Thad was asked if he wanted pain meds from the nurse when she came in. It was Belle that answered for him that he did. Then she and Maria climbed into the bed with him, and they snuggled up. Like they'd been doing since this nightmare began. Thad had never been so happy about having someone looking over them as he was right now. He thought they might be all right with Mr. Gibb and his brothers.

~*~

Dave looked at the two men that he had thought were following him. Turns out they were just as lost as he was. Moving slowly down the street, like there was any other way to move on this main drag, he thought about his next move. Then his mind, as it usually did about now, was back to where he'd shot his sister.

He thought that he'd gotten off two good shots at her. In his way of thinking, she should have been dead. However, he didn't know. Because every time he called the hospital for an update, they'd tell him they couldn't give out any information unless he had a code that was given out for patient privacy. So he'd had to make other arrangements about finding out what the hell she was doing still living. Not that any of his plans had worked so far. But he needed to get her out of the way. Anyway possible. Those kids were his, and he was going to take them as soon as he was able to kill off Maddy.

Surely, he told himself as he made his way through the hospital that she'd be on life support or something. But once he figured out she was on a surgical floor, he knew she'd been operated on. However, he could never get close enough to her room or what he thought would be her room because there were guards standing outside of it.

They wouldn't tell him shit, either. Even after offering them a bundle of cash that he didn't have didn't even get them to say a word to him. It was like they were mute or something. Nurses either. It was like they knew he was there to check on his sister and kept their records close to them.

Today he was going to try and sound off a fire alarm. He figured everyone would leave the place, leaving the sick and bedridden behind to burn up if it were a real fire. But then he'd be able to get into her room, if it was hers and finish what he had started. As he got off the elevator, he noticed a woman standing there whom he thought he'd seen before. Moving by her, she said his name. Dave turned to look at her.

"You do know me, idiot. I'm the one that was there when you tried to kill off your baby sister." He told her that he didn't know what she was talking about. "Sure you don't. Anyway, you're going to have to think up another plan other than the fire threat. I'm afraid I've taken precautions that will not allow you to scare a bunch of people for no reason."

"Again, I haven't any idea what you're talking about." She only grinned at him. "You think you know something? Spill it so that I can think it's funny too."

"Okay. It'll be my pleasure to let you in on a few things that we know about you. Your nieces and nephew have told the police what you were doing with them when you took them from their mom. Also, I know that you killed Nathan when he was trying to get money from your buddy Burney. Don't you want your family to have the basic needs of a home to go to and food on the table? There are also ten unexplained but now explained missing people that the police in your town know that you've killed. Thanks to me, they know where their bodies are now too. Had you been able to kill Maddy, you wouldn't have gotten what you wanted. It might interest you to know that your plan of them coming to you once their mother is dead isn't going to fly. Not so long as I have breath in my body. And there isn't any way that you can kill me. I'm immortal. Also, the kids won't be going anywhere near you, I'm afraid. I have friends in high places that will stop you from going within five inches of them." He looked around to see if anyone had heard her. "You'll be happy, or perhaps not — I don't really give a shit — that the Feds are after you too. I'm sure you know that not paying your taxes is against the law. Also, murder, but you've hit the big time with not paying on your ill-gotten gains by stealing."

"Where do you get your information? Besides, I have no idea what you're talking about." He looked down the hall where the guard was still standing in front of the door. "Do you suppose he'll be able to stop me once I decide to go after my sister? Nothing will when I decide — and I will be the one deciding when she dies when I go after her. She's too stupid to be living anyway. Did you know that she never once asked her kids for any kind of help with money? I'd be pushing that button daily to get some cash. But she had to stick her nose in where it wasn't needed. My sister is a moron."

"You think so? I know for a fact that she's gotten

the better of you several times now. For an entire month, you had to lay low until you healed up from the cut she gave you." Dave touched the scar that he had on his cheek when Maddy had the audacity to try and kill him. "You should really have a look at the guard again, Davy boy. I don't think you're going to get by him with just a gun, do you?"

He turned to look at the man and nearly fell on his ass when he saw that great big lion that was there roar at him. Trying to back away from it as it took a few steps in his direction had him not just falling on his ass but nearly breaking his neck when he tried to crawl behind the nurse's station to hide.

Davy closed his eyes. He'd been doing that since he'd been a kid now that he thought about it. When danger or his father was coming after him, he'd close his eyes. He'd be smarter. He'd tell himself every time if he was able to see how close the danger was, but nope. He could never get his eyes to stay open.

"You can come back out now, Davy. He's a man again." He asked her how she'd done that. "To use your phrase, I don't know what you're talking about."

Dave stayed right where he was until he heard

her laughing. As it faded away, he realized that there was no one at the desk. Nor were there any others around on the floor. Standing up, he looked around for files but all he found were notes, all of them with his name on them, calling him a murderer.

Thinking that he'd pull the alarm anyway, he was ready to pull the white bar when he felt a gun at the back of his head. Turning slowly, with his hands up, he saw that he was alone and that no one was behind him but the lion guard. Turning back around, he touched the bar this time. A sort of shock, like he'd touched something metal washed over his hand. Then damned if he wasn't blown across the room from a bigger electrical shock. It pitched him back hard enough that he blacked out for a couple of seconds. Mother fuck, it hurt to hit the wall that hard.

No matter how many times he made his way to another fire alarm, he couldn't touch it without being tossed away. Even using pencils or pens, gloves even that he found wouldn't keep him from getting hurt. Damn it all to hell and back. That bitch was going to pay for what she did to him. Then he heard her laughter

"You'll be thrilled to know that I've been looking

through that tiny mind of yours. Speaking of which, you have a tiny dick too. Several women have told you that over the years, haven't they? Poor Davy of the tiny peter. I would almost feel sorry for, well not you. A big dick is essential when trying to have a good time between the sheets, as they say." He asked her where she was. *"Like I'm going to be telling you anything like that. You really are a moron, aren't you? But as I was saying, I have a lot more information about your misdeeds than I did before. I'm making a list and having the police check on them. They don't even care that they're years old. They're so happy to have the cases closed that they could — well, they won't kiss you. Not with me telling them the things that you've done. "*

"You have nothing. You're a liar." She laughed, a sound that he was beginning to loathe. Then she told him how he'd killed his parents. *"So what? No one cared about them. No one even showed up at their funeral."*

"Because they were and still are terrified of you. When you got caught robbing the local grocery store, they threw a huge party in your dishonor. Imagine being hated so much that they had a party because you were taken to prison." He told her that they paid for that too. *"Yes, they did. You killed the mayor and his family for being the family that*

hosted it. They're currently exhuming their bodies as we speak. Along with your parents and your older sister. Did you really kill her because she wouldn't make you pasta at four in the morning? Not very nice of you. But then I guess once you start killing off family members killing off your other sister to gain control of her children wouldn't be a far stretch for you, now would it?"

"*I think that you're full of shit. That's what I think.*" She told him that she knew for a fact that he had killed his family off. "*Not about that. I have no idea how you know that shit, but it's not going to do you a bit of good. Once I have the kids, I'm going to make sure that I have enough money to pay you off.*"

"*Bullshit.*" He asked her what that was supposed to mean. "*I would have thought that you'd know that that meant Davy of the tiny peter. It's usually associated with a stupid or untrue talk or writing. You know, nonsense.*"

"*I know what the hell the word means, you bitch. I meant, what did you mean by saying it. That I'm not going to get the kids, which I will. Or that I'm going to have enough cash to pay everyone, including you off before I'm finished.*" She said that she was untouchable. "*No one is untouchable. You have a price, and I'm going to meet it.*

Then we'll see how I don't get the kids."

"I haven't any idea what you're were saying just *then."* He didn't either, but he wasn't going to admit that to her. She knew too much already. *"Enough of you emptying your brain to hear your own voice. I am the grand witch of all witches. I command that you will no longer lie to anyone, be they friend or foe. You will tell the truth to anyone that asks anything of you for the rest of your days. Going forth, you will no longer harm anyone. If you do, then you will get ten times the pain given back to you. If you cause a death to someone, you will die and come back ten times, each death more horrific than the last. You are doomed, David Winchester Farley, for the rest of your hopefully short life."*

It felt as if he'd been sucked through a small tube and brought out the other side being turned inside out. Once he was able to get over the feeling, his head started to explode in pain. His ears hurt, and he found blood on his hands when he held onto his head. Leaning over, he threw up three times before he felt like his stomach was going to be the next thing he tossed up from his throat. Since he was still in the hospital, he made his way to the emergency department to have them check him out. He'd never been so sick in his entire life.

"Do you need to be seen?" The woman across from him was going to get smacked for asking that of him when he was standing there looking like he'd bleed himself to death. "Mister? Do you need to be seen by a doctor?"

"Yes, you moron. I'm bleeding out of my ears. What do you think I want?" She told him to check his attitude at the door or she'd be checking him. "Whatever. Yes, I need to be seen. This woman put some kind of curse on me, and now I can't lie to anyone. She also is going to turn me over to the police or something."

"Well aren't you full of good news? What a nice person to do that for us. All right, tell me your name and birthdate." After giving her all the information she asked of him, he was told to have a seat and that someone would be with him soon.

"No, I need to be seen right away. Didn't I just tell you that I'm cursed with something and that she made my ears bleed?" She just stared at him. "I demand that you see me right now."

"I do see you right now. You're making an ass of yourself by standing right in front of me. Now, sit down if you want to be seen, or I'll have security escort you out of here. Sit."

He did. Right on the fucking floor. Then when the woman and the others started laughing at him, he stood up and made his way to the waiting area. This shit was going to stop soon, or he was going to have to take action. He hadn't any idea what that might be, but he wasn't going to be the laughingstock of a fucking hospital. When he found a place far away from the rest of the people in the area, Dave counted how many people were ahead of him. Christ, he was going to be here forever, for the amount of people that were seated in the lobby.

He was going to find that bitch and make her pay. Whatever she'd done to him, it was something that he didn't care for, and she was going to take it back. Right before he killed her. Dave thought that he might enjoy killing her more than he did anyone before. He was going to make her suffer too.

Chapter 8

Frazier felt the bed move under him and reached for Amelia. When she moaned, he let her get comfy by wrapping herself around him. Holding her, just wrapping his arms around her, made him feel like the world was less cold and that he had someone in his corner for the rest of his life.

"Dave has been arrested for causing a scene in the hospital. Someone got to go to a room before he did, and that pissed him off something terrible." Amelia giggled. "He really is a moron of the first degree. Anyway, so far, the police in every town that he's been in has a list of the people that he killed. If I didn't have a name for them, I could at least send them to find the body. How was your day?"

"Better than yours, I think." She told him that she was having fun getting all the information on Dave so that he'd be sentenced for several lifetimes. "Then I guess we both had a good day. I got most of the smaller pieces in the table in resin. And the few pieces that are part of the mountain here are dried enough that I'll be able to put them in the work too."

"I can't wait to see it finished. I bet it'll be epic once it's shined up and complete." He told her that he hoped so. She rolled over him and straddled his hips. Her legs on either side of him made his cock stretch. "You need to be more confident. Your Grannie told me that you did have little faith in your work. From what I've seen, you should be doing it full-time."

"I want to. I don't know if I could do it full-time. I need to be out in the open, too, a great deal. But I'm not going back to work full-time at any job. Especially not the Park." She said she understood. "I thought you might. It's lost its appeal to me. What with grandda being killed and grannie leaving us...I don't know. I might go back someday but not right away. Time.

I want to spend more time just being me and doing things that I enjoy." He moved his hips and felt her pussy at his balls. "Like making love to you whenever I want. Wanna ride my cock, my lovely mate?"

When she got up on her knees, Frazier held his cock so she could lower herself over him. As soon as she took him into her body, her dark hot sheath, he felt his eyes roll to the back of his head. Christ, she was wonderfully wet.

Amelia kept pushing his hands away when he wanted to pull her down atop of him. Instead, she took her time riding him, even going to far as to slide her fingers down to her pussy and play with herself. It was nearly too much for him. Frazier wanted to fuck her so badly that he sat up and pulled her mouth to his.

He fucked her mouth with his tongue. Made love to her body with his hands. Frazier wanted, no, he needed so much more. Rolling her to her back, he nearly came when she wrapped her legs around his and then slid them up to his hips. He wasn't sure he was going to last until she offered her breasts to him. It was all he could do not to cry out his climax and roar as it left his body. Even as he came a second time,

Frazier was so needy that he knew he had to have all of her.

Her body was firm beneath his hands. Her breasts, even as he suckled at them, filled his mouth. When her legs moved up and over his hips so that he was able to move deeper inside of her, he felt his bear move along his skin. She was in heat. Pulling his mouth away, just long enough to get her attention, he told her.

"If we haven't already created a child, we will now." She told him to fill her. To give her his child.

It was as if she had given him everything in the world when she begged him to give her their baby. Slowing down just a little, he touched her everywhere his hands could reach. It still wasn't enough. He needed her all, everything that she could give him. Moving his mouth to her throat, he licked the pounding pulse, tasted her need, the sweet sweat of her flesh and bit down.

He'd bitten her before, but this time was different. The connection between the two of them had always been strong, but it was almost as if they were a single entity. They were one. And in that moment, the clarity of their union moved into his sight. Their child, a beautiful little girl with dark curly hair and beautiful blue eyes, looked up at him.

"Now, Frazier." The vision disappeared, and he found himself coming deeply in Amelia. As his balls emptied, they filled again and again until he knew he was going to be sore from it come morning.

Her nails dug deeply into his back; blood streamed down his rib as she cried out that she was coming. Feeling her body tightening around his cock, made him come again, quick heart-pounding climaxes that made him dizzy with exhaustion.

When he woke, he hadn't any idea where he was. The room was bright with light and the bed was in the wrong place. Sitting up, careful of the way his head was spinning, he looked around and saw Amelia.

Dressed all in white, she was nursing a child. Their child. Frazier watched as she cooed to her. Telling her that she was the apple of her eye and that the earth had blessed her with a great deal of magic.

Holding onto his head when the room began to spin again, he saw a little girl standing at the window, This time in another bedroom. He could see in front of her the snow drifting down from the sky. When she turned to him, he could see that this was a different child. Her eyes were as brown as his were. But she looked so much like her mother that he knew her to be his and Amelia's.

When the room changed again, this time to the kitchen of his grandparent's home, he saw a woman there. One that he'd never met before now. When his brother Barron walked to her, putting his hand on her swollen belly, he knew that this would be the last time he would see him in a while. They were the ones that were leaving the mountain.

Frazier opened his eyes and sat up in the bed. He was home, in the present time. Looking for Amelia, he found her in the bathroom. She was brushing her teeth and humming a tune that he'd not heard since he'd been a child.

"I just had the most incredible dreams." She only smiled at him. "You saw them too? You know what I saw?"

"No. You have a lot more magic than you did before. Do you want to tell me what you saw?" He did, but he also didn't want to share just yet. "You don't have to. I know that you will someday, but not today.

Correct?"

Instead of answering her, he kissed her. She was his life, and they were going to have a child. Several if his dreams were true. Getting to his knees, he removed the towel she'd wrapped around her after her shower. Kissing her still flat belly, he hugged her there as well, putting his ear to where he knew his little girl was safely cocooned.

"It's a girl. I don't know why I know that just now but we're having a little girl." He nodded, his emotions getting the better of him, the longer he held her. "I'd like to name her after your grannie. And my mom."

"Granny's first name was Alma middle was Millicent. She went by Minnie because her mother was Alma. I think my grandda's middle name was Alford, and his first name was Peter, after his grandda." She said she'd take care that their son was named for him as well. "What is your mom's name? I don't think I ever knew."

"Beatrice Anna. I don't know that she had a last name. When pressed about a last name, I'd just come up with something that was around the room, like a book title or an author. For a very long time, I just used Becker. So what do you think about Millicent Anna? Or Beatrice Alma?" He looked up at her. "I'm up for either of them. I really like them both."

"I do as well. We'll use one for this child, and if we have another girl, we'll use the other. That should be good enough, right?" She told him what she wanted to call their son. "Peter Frazier? I think I like that name very much. We'll call him Pete."

"Yes, perfect." Frazier stood up and kissed her again. "I really need to get going. I don't want to, but I have about a million things to get finished today. In addition to Dave, I have to figure out what is being done about the witches' council, and I have to find someone that is willing to be my right-hand man. I was thinking of asking Sunny to be there for me. Sort of like someone to hold my temper at bay when I need it."

"She'd love it. But why do you need a council?" She said that she didn't. "Then why bother. It's not like they're going to be very helpful to you since you pretty much rule it all. Just don't bother. It will only be one more thing for you to have to mess with, and with a baby coming along, it might be more headache than it's worth."

When she said that she'd think about it, he was happy. Taking a shower made him think about how sore he was, and he couldn't be the least bit upset about how bending to pick up the soap had made him whimper. At least he wouldn't have to explain to Amelia why he was whining like a baby.

Heading out to his building, he was just getting the resin measured out when Maria joined him. He'd forgotten that the kids were out of the hospital and asked her if Gibb knew where she was. Frazier told her she needed to be careful, too, because of the wild animals that roamed the land.

"Mr. Gibb told me to be extra careful. He knows that I was coming here." She didn't touch anything he had laying out but did answer her questions that she had about things. "I love to work with paint. We haven't been anywhere that I could play around with it. Do you think that Mr. Gibb would mind if I asked him for some?"

"No, he'd be thrilled. However, you're welcome to come out here and use what I have so long as you clean up after yourself when you're finished." She turned and looked at him wide-eyed. "What? You expected me to tell you to stay out of here and leave my things alone? I'd never do that. Not to anyone wanting to create. You can come here when you wish, but make sure that someone knows where you are. Like I said, it could be dangerous."

"I promise you that I'll take care of things." It only took him a few minutes to set her up with some watercolors. She said that was what she used at home. He also showed her where the canvas was that she could use. Again, he cautioned her about using the machine to stretch and make a canvas for her to use. "This is really nice of you, Mr. Frazier. I can't thank you enough."

"If you want to call me something, call me either Frazier or Uncle Frazier. You were told that your mom is Gibb's mate, right?" She nodded as she picked out a brush to use. "Good. I'm going to be working over here. I sometimes get caught up in my work, so don't be surprised that I might not answer you right away. All right?"

"Yes, all right. I do the same thing. I'll let you know if I leave or something." As she set to work, he did as well. He was finished mixing the resin and pouring it when he realized that he was enjoying having her out here with him. She wasn't a chatterbox like most people would be but buried her head into what she was doing and looked to be having fun.

The touch to his shoulder had him turning quickly. It was Maria, and she was smiling at him. When he asked her if she was all right, she smiled bigger and asked him if he wanted anything from the house. That she was going to get her a snack.

"I have some out here. Water, too, if you want it." After getting them both a couple of granola bars and a bottle of water, he looked at her painting. "Christ, honey. That's fantastic."

It was too. Walking closer to the little girl's art, he was blown away by her mastery of the paintbrush. Sitting in front of the work, he marveled at the talent one so young had. Frazier asked if Gibb had seen her work.

"No. I mean, I didn't want to bother him with the paint and things until my mom came home. But then I saw you coming out here and thought that—do you really like it?" He reached for his brother, telling him to get out there as soon as he could. Then he told her how much he loved it. "Thank you so much. I think that I've not been this relaxed in a while. It felt good to be able to do something again that is normal."

He hugged her tightly when she started to tear up, and he was still holding her when not just Gibb showed up but Mark and Ewing as well. They thought that he'd done it and was so happy to tell them and surprise them that little Maria had done it. He knew that she was going to be going places, and he was thrilled beyond words that he got to help her even just a little to get going on her art again.

~*~

It was nearly midnight when Amelia got back to the house. Her body was aching, and she was so tired, but she had gotten a great deal of work done today and was proud of it. Frazier was in the dining room with several catalogs lying around him. She picked up one and read the company name.

"Thinking of adding more supplies to your work?" He laughed with her and told her about the art that Maria had done. He handed her his phone to show her a picture he'd taken. "That's wonderful. So you're going to buy her some supplies? That's nice of you."

"Gibb asked me to figure out what she'd need. The problem is, I want to get her everything all at once. But I know that I can't do that. Also, I don't think that I should just get her some things to work with. I need to make sure that the other two have things they can work on as well." She sat down beside him. "You think that I'm nuts, don't you?"

"No. I think that our children are going to be spoiled rotten if you don't reign your need to please in a bit." They both laughed, and he kissed her. "Ask them what they want to do. Have space for them in your place for them to come and go as they want. The house too. I know they don't live all that far away, but it would be good if they had spaces to go when they need some time alone."

"I like that. I know that growing up with my brothers around all the time, it was hard to get a moment to myself. I think that's why I went out here to work. Well, not that building but one that sat here before the one I have now." He smiled at her. "You've had a rough day, haven't you? I can tell that you're stressed too."

"I did. I decided you were right about the council and didn't bother with that. Sunny said she'd love to be there for me; however, she suggested I ask Jamie, too, as she wasn't as hot-headed as she was. I think she made an excellent point, and the three of us had lunch to discuss the things that I'd need." Amelia laughed. "I had to go to another coven to break up a horrific fight. They were being pissy with their leader over some of the food that was brought to the meeting. That is the reason that I never supply food. Everyone is never happy about what is being served."

"I know that. When we're all together, we usually have Chinese food. It's all of our favorites. And the fact that we can get several dishes of each kind we all like helps a great deal as well." She told him that she had noticed that there were never any leftovers. "Leftovers? What are those?"

She loved being able to unwind with Frazier. He could get her not thinking about her day in no time at all. She felt like her day wasn't nearly as bad as she'd thought and could go to bed with the assurances that she was going to sleep well. And she would too. With him beside her.

"I've been working on some things around the barn and have run across a few pieces of furniture I'd like to somehow get here. One of the things is the mantel that was in the original part of the house. It's huge, but I think with the size of our fireplace, it will look good." They put the things away and headed up the stairs while Frazier continued about his afternoon. "Gibb was with me, and he's going to take a couple of the beds that have been stored there. He asked the kids if they wanted them, and the girls took them both. He will have to get a mattress made for the beds as they're an odd size. But Thad took one of the bigger beds that we found. I think it might be bigger than a king-sized bed. In order for him to be able to use it, he's going to have to switch rooms around. The kid wanted to do it right then, but he was holding back. I'm guessing that he didn't want to be a burden or something. So we called the others in and got him all situated."

"You're a great uncle to them. And you're going to be a wonderful father." He said that he hoped so. "You will be. I know it."

Getting into bed, she realized just how exhausted

she was. Even if the house had been on fire, she was sure she couldn't have made it out. Almost as soon as her head hit the pillow, she was out. Her mother picked that time to contact her.

"Why do you have to be around when I'm exhausted?" Her mom laughed. *"All right. Tell me what you need to and leave me alone. I'm too tired to be nice to you right now."*

"You are rarely nice to anyone. Well, that's not true. You are nicer since you and Frazier are a couple. I have some news for you. Good news." She asked her if it could have waited until the morning to tell her. *"You're receptive to hearing from me when you're asleep. Now listen to me. There is a man that is making inquiries about a coven of witches. You need to make sure that he is aware that you're not going to be putting up with his shit."*

"What does he want? And mom, so you know, that's not what I'd call good news. Sort of shitty news if you ask me." Mom told her that he wanted to burn them out of existence. *"Are you kidding me? Who the hell does that shit anymore. I'm thinking that he has a little following, and it's gone to his head."*

"He has a large following. Several thousand people are playing into his nonsense. His theory is that witches are

the cause of all the strife in the world and that they made shifters to take over the world of decent folks. I wonder if he realizes that he isn't one of the decent folks? More than likely, he thinks his bloodline is pure. Idiot. He has several shifters in his bloodline, and while I haven't made much in the way of contact with his mind, I think that he might have this shit going on because he's a shifter himself. But I don't know. My magic is diminished somewhat since I came to rest." She asked her mom if she knew how she was to deal with him. *"I'm not sure other than to call him out. As I said, my magic isn't what it used to be."*

"All right. I'll see what I can find out in the morning. What is his name?" She told her. *"Brian Wilcox? Why does that sound familiar?"*

"I don't know. You have a look for him and —"

"He's the guy that lived in the house next to that coven leader. What was her name? It'll come to me. She wanted his house. I can see this happening. The guy is getting back — damn it, I ruled in their favor too. What the fuck, mom? What is his beef with witches?" She said that she didn't know. *"I'm going to have to pay him a little visit, I guess. I'll take Sunny and Jamie with me so I don't just turn him into something that will haunt him for years. How the hell*

did he get so many followers in such a short amount of time anyway?"

"I would assume that he was getting pissy with the witches if what you say about his neighbor has any bearing on things. He's probably been on social media things and has bitched about them for all the time it was getting resolved. That sounds like as good a reason as any." She agreed with her. *"All right. Now that I've worked you into a lather, I'll let you go. I won't be able to help you with this, but I want you to know that with the last bonding that you and Frazier had, it really zapped the world around witches. Also, I'm so happy that you're going to have a child. I could just do a happy dance. I'm so happy."*

After her mom closed the connection, she felt like she needed to get up and start on her day. At least look up some things about Wilcox that she could use against him. But Frazier turned to her and pulled her into his arms, and she felt at peace. Not just to go to sleep but at peace all over her body. Curling around him, she let herself surrender to sleep and felt like she could conquer the world then.

Waking up in the morning, she was alone in the big bed. Looking at the alarm clock, she saw a note there with her name on it. Picking it up, she realized that it was from Frazier, and it occurred to her that she'd never seen his handwriting before. Opening the note up, she smiled when she read the first line.

"My darling wife. Good morning. I'm going to the meeting you had this morning with the coven in West Virginia. Sunny and Dexter are going with me as they have some places that they want to look into. I'm not sure what that entails, but they're happy to be with me." She sat up more in the bed as she continued reading. "I've placed an order that is to be delivered sometime this afternoon. Gibb is going to come over when you get it so that he can pick it up. I've taken your advice, and I've got with the other two kids, and they're going to work in the building with Maria. They will be one hell of a talented family if they are even half as good as their sister. Maddy is doing well. They expect to take her out of the coma sometime tomorrow. We're all going to be there for her when she wakes. I'm sure that you know it's going to go well. I have to get going. You look so wonderful lying there, all peaceful in sleep. I love you with all my heart." Then he signed it, Frazier.

Getting up, she had her shower and was ready to get her day going when the front doorbell rang. It was the delivery guy, and she wasn't the least bit surprised when there were several boxes of products being delivered. What did surprise her was the fact that the kids, when they came over, knew more about the things that had come than she did. Thad was more than a little excited about the polymer clay that had been in the boxes than anything else.

After helping with the breakdown of the boxes, she found herself alone in the big house. Deciding that it was the perfect time to get out and find some of the herbs that she'd been wanting to dry, Amelia set off for the mountain.

In her element of doing things that she loved, she was surprised when she realized that she'd skipped lunch in favor of her walk. But her basket was full, and she couldn't have been more happy. As she made her way back down the hill, she was startled out of her thoughts when a gunshot sounded in the woods around her. She was just able to duck around a tree when three men came out of the darkening forest near her.

"I know that I saw that woman. They're all up here doing their voodoo shit." One of the men with him said that was another cult altogether. "Whatever. Just help me look for her body. I know that I was able to hit her."

"I don't think this is such a good idea." The man holding the rifle told the other man to shut his trap. "No, I don't think so. I'm going to go home. I thought you were only going to talk to her. I'm not going down for the murder of something that I knew nothing about."

"You leave, and you're out of the club." The man turned and said that he didn't want to be in it anyway. "You bastard, get back here. I'm going to need some help burying the body."

"I don't think so." She hit the man with her fist and was happy to watch him turning head over ass as he rolled down the hill. Reaching out to the others, she told them what was going on. Just as one of the brothers came running up the hill as his bear, she laughed when the man, more than likely Wilcox, started screaming like a little girl. "You're going to jail, dumbass. I hope you rot in there."

She didn't know how the police got there so quickly, but she was happy to see the end of the man. The second and third man went to the station to tell their side of the story while she was able to stay home and have the interview there. Amelia wondered if life on the mountain was going to be like this all the time. An adventure daily.

Before You Go...

HELP AN AUTHOR

write a review

THANK YOU!

Share your voice and help guide other readers to these wonderful books. Even if it's only a line or two, your reviews help readers discover the author's books so they can continue creating stories that you'll love. Log in to your favorite retailer and leave a review. Thank you.

AWARD WINNING, BESTSELLING AUTHOR

Kathi Barton, a winner of the Pinnacle Book Achievement Award and a best-selling author on Amazon and All Romance books, lives in Nashport, Ohio, with her husband, Paul. When not creating new worlds and romance, Kathi and her husband enjoy camping and going to auctions. She can also be seen at county fairs with her husband, an artist and potter.

Her muse, a cross between Jimmy Stewart and Hugh Jackman, brings her stories to life for her readers in a way that has them coming back time and again for more. Her favorite genre is paranormal romance, with a great deal of spice. You can visit Kathi online and drop her an email if you'd like. She loves hearing from her fans. aaronskiss@gmail.com.

Follow Kathi on her blog: http://kathisbartonauthor.blogspot.com/

www.ingramcontent.com/pod-product-compliance
Lightning Source LLC
Chambersburg PA
CBHW030222180626
46810CB00008B/2931